A FALSE FRONT

THE BUILDERS, BOOK 2

VANESSA GRAY BARTAL

DRY CREEK PRESS

Copyright © 2021 by Vanessa Gray Bartal

All rights reserved.

No part of this book may be reproduced in any form or by any electronic or mechanical means, including information storage and retrieval systems, without written permission from the author, except for the use of brief quotations in a book review.

❀ Created with Vellum

CHAPTER 1

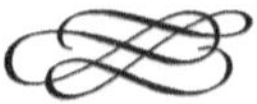

"Benny, I have some bad news."

Benedict Samperi looked up at his secretary with a smile. She was a good secretary, the capable sort who kept to herself, unless there was something she knew she couldn't handle alone.

"What's the problem, Molly?"

"The Lawton group pulled out of the project."

Benny's hands tightened into fists on his keyboard. He moved them under the table where Molly couldn't see. "Thank you, Molly. I'll look into it." With a nod, she let herself out and closed the door. Benny sat staring into space a long time after she left. Their company, Samperi Builders, did a fair amount of charity work in the community. At Benny's behest, they had also recently instigated a mission team headed to an Appalachian community to repair tornado damage. The project was being entirely funded by the Lawton group, until today. But why?

You know why.

He would have to go there, to try and make amends that were long overdue. Like a child, he stubbornly resisted. It had been years since the incident. Could it really still have this much of an effect on his life and the lives of those around him? *Yes.* Still, he put it off as long as he could, until the end of the day.

"Where are you heading off to?" his brother Joe asked as Benny stepped out of his office and turned toward the exit.

"The Lawton group. They pulled the funding for the project," Benny said.

"What?" His sister, Jessamine, poked her head out of the meeting room. It was Benny's luck the one day he had to eat crow was the one day his family all happened to be in the office. Usually they were out working on a job. But today, the last day of the month before payroll, they were in to check their budgets. People thought the Samperis were successful because there were so many of them. The truth was because they were meticulous, paying special attention to the details and always keeping an eye on budgets and deadlines.

"I'm going to go talk to them," Benny said.

"I'm sure you'll get it worked out," Joe said unconcernedly and Jessamine disappeared back where she came from. Usually that might have been true. Benny had a way of getting people to give him money for things. Before he got malaria and had to come home, he had been the Chief Operating Officer and fundraiser for the entire South American division of the charity he represented. But that was then and this was now, and no one but Benny knew what he knew about his history with the Lawton group.

Benny didn't answer. He had too much on his mind. He drove slowly across town, half hoping they would be closed by the time he arrived. But they weren't. After identifying himself to the receptionist, he sat in the lobby and waited to be seen. He had to wait a long time, and then at last his name was called. He found, as he stood, his legs were a little wobbly, his stomach a little queasy. The malaria still lingered in his system, but that wasn't a problem today. It was nerves. He had sat across from billionaires to ask for money, from third world despots to ask for mercy, and not felt as anxious as he felt today. When had he last been nervous about anything? He couldn't remember. But the anticipation of the upcoming meeting had him quaking.

The receptionist opened the door to the inner sanctum. Benny stepped inside the plush office, his eyes roaming over the wood paneling and leather before settling on the person behind the desk. She looked good, the best he'd ever seen her. The short blond bob she'd harbored in high school had grown to long, lush locks. What he could see of her from the waist up behind her massive desk looked sleek and toned, as if she spent a lot of time and effort on staying in shape. But he refused to let his approval register on his face because she'd know it, and she would use it against him.

"Hello, Lou." He slouched into one of the overstuffed chairs opposite her desk, feigning far more ease than he felt.

"Hello, Ben. Have a seat," she said, the hint of sarcasm in her tone intending to chastise him for not waiting for an invitation.

"You're looking good," he said, ignoring the intended barb.

She nodded slightly in acknowledgement, her eyes raking him up and down. She was thinking he did not look good, and he agreed. The malaria had ravaged him, inside and out, leaving him gaunt, pallid, and weak.

"What brings you here today, Benny?" she asked. Her accent was refined and far gentler than the woman herself.

"I think you know," he said. His accent tended more toward Brooklyn, though more than a hint of Kentucky had seeped in over the years. Like his parents, the New York became more defined when he was upset. Right now his consonants were clipped; he worked to relax them.

"Do I?" Her pen rested lightly between lips stretched into a sardonic smile.

"Are we going to play games, Lou, or are we going to have it out in the open?" he said. "You're still mad at me, and that's fine. But you're taking it out on innocent people, and that's not right."

She set the pen down on the table, hard. "Not right? Who are you to lecture me about what's not right?"

"I'm the person who's leading this team, a team that's going to help impoverished children," he said. He was finding it hard to keep a cap on his temper, and that surprised him. After all he had seen, very few things got under his skin. And it wasn't as if Lou didn't have a right to hate him. She had every right, and then some.

She rolled her eyes. "St. Benedict, off to save the world one tornado ravaged town at a time."

Don't call me that. The words were almost out of his mouth before he reeled them back. He wouldn't give her the satisfaction of knowing how much he hated to be called a saint. "No man is a saint," he said instead.

She snorted an indelicate laugh. "That's an ironic thing for you to say."

He wanted to leave, to turn around and excuse himself from her anger and loathing. But the trip was too important; there were too many people counting on him and her money. "Why did you fund the trip in the first place?" he asked.

"Because I didn't know you were home," she said.

"You have no problem with the rest of my family," he clarified.

"Exactly. Let one of them lead the trip, and I'll give back the money," she said.

"No."

"Then you're not getting a dime."

"Grow up, Lou, you're being ridiculous," he said.

She shrugged. "Ridiculous or not, it's my money, and I can do what I want with it."

"Of all the heartless, selfish people I've met, you might top the list," he said. It had been a long time since he had been well and truly angry with anyone. He had been told his anger was a formidable thing, and for that reason he barely used it. Lou, however, seemed unfazed.

"I guess it takes a heartless, selfish person to know one," she said.

"You didn't used to be like this," he said.

"And you always were," she said.

"What do you want from me?" he asked, exasperated.

"I want you to be unmasked; I want the rest of the world to know what I've always known—St. Benedict is a big, fat fraud," she said. Two red spots of color stained her cheeks, and Benny knew they had nothing to do with the expensive makeup she was wearing.

"Ridiculous. I should have known I wouldn't be able to have a rational conversation with someone like you," he said.

"What do you mean someone like me?" she asked.

"Someone who uses her money and power like a weapon," he said.

"At least I'm upfront about it. I don't pretend to be nice when I'm not," she said.

He stood. "What happened between us happened when we were kids. We're adults now, and you're going to have to live with this on your conscience. Good luck, Lou." He turned and let himself out of her office before she could respond.

Lou watched him go with a mixture of relief and disappointment. She had been hoping for more—more of a reaction, more deference, more arguing.

She had come a long way since high school, practically light years from the lonely, deluded creature she had been. She wanted, no *needed*, Benny to acknowledge that. But he hadn't, drat him. She had also wanted to hear his long-delayed apology, and maybe a bit of groveling. But that hadn't come, either. Failing all of that, she had wanted to have one, big, unending row with him. She wanted him to yell and throw things, to beg her for the money, if that was what it took. But of course he hadn't done that either. Benedict Samperi had never, ever given Lou what she wanted, and he never would. When would she learn?

She sniffled a little and pressed her fingers to her eyes, refusing to let the tears flow. She hadn't cried about him in years; she had no intention of starting now.

Was it safe to leave? She hoped so. The day had been long, even before Benny's arrival. Her legs ached. She reached down to rub the tender skin around her braces, wanting nothing more than to go home and take them off. They helped her walk, but not without a price. In a weird way the constant, nagging pain had become a sort of friend. She used it to drive her, to remind herself how far she'd come and realize how far she had to go.

He had to be gone by now. It had been almost ten minutes. She stood and walked to the cupboard to retrieve her purse. When she was fully rested and the day was new, she could hide her limp. But other times, like now when she was tired, her foot dragged slightly behind like an errant toddler. There was no faking it, no trying to pretend away her condition.

Her phone was in her hand as she limped to the lobby. Her head was down, checking messages. That was why she didn't see him until she almost ran into him. She reached the elevator and stopped short, Benny only a foot away.

"Oh," she said stupidly.

"Your elevator is slow," he said. He had calmed considerably, and she hated that. Emotion was power. As long as he was displaying it, she had the upper hand. But now that he was mellow, she aimed to mimic his tone.

"It's a long way up," she said. Her office was on the 30th floor, making her building the tallest one in the town where she worked. In the small town next door, where she and Benny lived, the town where they had grown up and gone to school together, nothing had more than two floors.

Finally the bell dinged and the door opened. Benny stepped inside and put his hand in front of the sensor, halting it. "Are you able to share an elevator with me, or is that too much for your delicate sensibilities?"

Ignoring him, she stepped inside. He pushed the button for the ground floor. The door closed, and the unthinkable happened. With the snap of a cable, the elevator broke free and started to plummet.

CHAPTER 2

Neither Lou nor Benny made a sound, but they did reach for each other, instinctively and simultaneously. Lou nestled her face against his chest and Benny rested his head protectively on hers, waiting for an impact that never came.

After about fifteen agonizing, terrifying seconds, the elevator came to a sudden and jarring halt. Benny and Lou were tossed haphazardly to the ground. She bashed her shoulder against the wall and Benny groaned. The lights went out. Everything was black for a minute before the emergency lights flicked dimly awake.

"Are you all right?" Benny asked. He sounded as shaken as she felt.

"I think so," Lou said. Her legs hurt, but then they always did. Her shoulder hurt, too, but more like a bruise than a break. In the dim light, she saw Benny reach up and push the emergency button. "No one's here to hear it," she said. She had sent everyone home, not wanting anyone to be privy to her meeting with Ben.

"You never know," said Benny, ever the optimist.

Gingerly, Lou sat up and reached for her phone. It wasn't in her pocket. The fall had tossed it across the elevator. She crawled to it like a lifeline, but it was hopelessly smashed. "Do you have your phone?" she asked.

"I don't have a cell phone," he said.

"What kind of person doesn't have a cell phone?" she snapped.

"The kind who's been living in the jungle for the past three years," he replied, equally as terse. "I'm fine, by the way. Thanks for asking."

"Of course you're fine," she said. *For now.* Who knew how much longer they could dangle this way? The elevator could plummet again at any moment, this time to the ground.

Benny stood and tried to pry apart the elevator doors, but they wouldn't budge. Frustrated, he paused and wiped his brow. He was sweating profusely, much more than Lou was. "Why are you in a flop sweat?" she asked, fully intending to be as mean as she felt, despite the direness of their situation.

"Gee, Lou, it's almost like I have malaria or something," he said.

"You don't have to take it out on me. I'm not the mosquito or monkey that bit you," she said.

He sank to the floor. "You're right. I'm frustrated because I don't like being weak."

"I'm weak, and you don't see me getting all huffy about it," she said. When he didn't respond, she poked him with her foot. "That was a joke, Samperi."

He caught her foot and held it aloft, inspecting one of her braces. She tried not to squirm self-consciously during his inspection. "I was wondering how you're walking now. Are you bionic?"

"More like Darth Vader," she said.

"You look good, Lou," he said.

"It's Hattie now, actually," she said primly.

He dropped her foot and shook his head.

"What?" she pressed.

"Your name has always been Hattie Lou and everyone has always called you Lou."

"Now I want everyone to call me Hattie," she said.

"I'm not calling you that," he said.

"It's my name," she said.

"Don't be one of those people," he said.

"One of what people?" she asked.

"One of those people who feels the need to reinvent everything all the time. You're Lou. You always have been, you always will be, and there's nothing wrong with that."

"Ding, ding, ding. Our session's over. Thank you, doctor. Here's your thousand dollars," she said.

"Is that what shrinks go for these days?" he asked.

"The good ones," she said.

"And you got all that wisdom for free. It's lucky we got trapped," he said. "By the way, it wasn't a monkey."

"What?" she asked, confused.

"The malaria. I've never been bitten by a monkey, for the record."

"Me, neither. It's nice we've found common ground again," she said. He smiled a genuine smile, and she had to look away. Even gaunt and jaundiced, he was a handsome man. She didn't want to be attracted to him, not anymore. That ship sailed a long time ago. In fact, it ran aground and burst into flames before being swallowed by a whale.

"What's in your purse?" he asked.

She clutched it closer. "Why?"

"Because I want to rob you. Why do you think? I was wondering if you have any snacks."

"Who carries snacks in their purse?" she asked.

"My mom," he said.

"Well, I'm fresh out of Cheerios and teething biscuits. The purse is leather, so you could gnaw on the strap, if you want," she offered.

"Maybe later," he said. "I don't suppose you have any card games or a pen and paper so we could play hangman."

"You could take off your pants and we could play real hangman," she said.

"Gee, Lou, you're in my presence for ten minutes and you're already trying to get my pants off," he said.

"You must get that a lot, women wanting to hang you from the rafters, I mean."

"Strangely, it hasn't happened in a while." He scooted closer so he was sitting beside her.

"What are you doing?" she asked.

"Easy there, bunny, I'm not going to hurt you," he gentled.

She could smell him now and, to her horror, she remembered the indelible scent of him. It was a primal thing, the intoxicating mix of his pheromones, and she didn't like it at all. "Seriously, what are you doing? Go back to your side."

"Look, Lou, this is a serious situation. I'd rather not be alone."

"You're not alone, but we don't have to be touching," she said.

"I would ask who hurt you, but we both know it was me," he said. Was it her imagination or did he sound a little sad?

"Let's not do this," she said.

"Do what?"

"Let's not dredge up the past and talk about our *feelings*. Gag. Let's act like two grownups who can weather a slight emergency with confidence and fortitude."

"You sound like a brochure for the boy scouts," he said. "Let's do something."

"Let's play the quiet game. You start," she said.

"I'm hungry and in need of distraction. Let's do something."

"What do you want to do? Count freckles?"

"We could make out," he suggested.

"So, I'm trapped in an elevator and you're trapped in a thirteen-year-old's brain. Are you genuinely mentally ill? First of all no one says 'make out' anymore. It's called hooking up. Or something, I don't know. But not making out. Second, what is wrong with you? No, seriously, what is your malfunction? We're in our thirties and we hate each other."

"I don't hate you," he said.

"We're still both in our thirties. We don't have slumber parties and seven minutes in heaven anymore," she said.

"Oh, I get it. I understand. Sorry."

His tone was patronizing. If there was one thing Lou couldn't abide, it was condescension. It was almost like he knew, but how could he? "What do you understand?" she said.

"You've never done this before," he said in the same aggravating tone.

"What? Been trapped in an elevator with a teenage boy trapped in a man's body? You've got me, this is a whole new, delightful experience," she said.

"You've never kissed anyone before. I get it. It's all right. Don't be embarrassed."

"I've kissed plenty of men, you monkey-plagued moron," she said.

"You never kissed anyone in high school, and you still haven't kissed anyone now," he declared.

"I kissed two people in high school. As far as who I've kissed after, it's none of your concern."

"Sure, Jan," he said, doing his best Marcia Brady impression. "Was his name George Glass?"

"No, try your cousin Mateo from Brooklyn," she said.

"What?" he exclaimed, well and truly shocked.

"You left the room to get something, and he laid one on me."

"How long was I out of the room?" he exclaimed.

"Long enough for me to kiss him back," she said. "And realize I liked it."

"You're lying," he said.

"Call him and ask him, oh, that's right, you share your love of technology with the Amish," she said.

"Why would you kiss my cousin? That's weird, that's like best friend cheating," he said.

"There's no law that says you can't kiss your best friend's cousin," she said.

"Yes, there is. It's called morals," he said.

"You're acting like a jealous person," she informed him.

"It's wrong and weird and you both kept it a secret, and that makes it weirder," he said.

"If it helps, it was nineteen years ago and, believe it or not, I've somehow been able to move on with my life," she said.

"Who was the other one?" he asked, fuming.

"Other one what?" she asked.

"Other kiss in high school. You said there were two," he reminded her. "Was it one of my brothers? My dad? My grandpa?"

"Everett Rains," she told him.

"The captain of the football team," he said.

"Do you know another guy with that name from our high school?" she asked.

"You are so totally and completely lying," he said.

"He works at the car dealership on the end of Main Street. Stop in and ask him sometime," she said. "Though, to be fair, he did it on a dare. It still counts, though."

"You want me to stop in to the place of work of a guy I haven't seen in twenty years and ask him if he kissed my best friend in high school on a dare?"

"How else are you going to know I'm telling the truth?" she asked.

"I'm going to use my vast powers of deduction." He squinted and put his fingers to his temple. "Done. You're lying."

"I am not, you fevered ogre," she said. "I've kissed literally more than a dozen men in my life, and I'm good at it. Really, really good."

"Mm, hmm. It's okay, Lou, really. You have nothing to prove here." He patted her hand. She jerked it away, sat up, and pressed her lips roughly to his before quickly pulling away.

"There, now shut up," she said.

"I'm not going to lie, Lou, that wasn't so good."

"Are you actually complaining about the way I kissed you? Because I do have a knife in my purse, and I'll cut you. It's dull, but I'll get the job done."

"That was an angry kiss. It was like your lips were taking revenge or something. That's not how this moment is supposed to work," he said.

"What moment? We are not having a moment," she said.

"We're trapped in an elevator together and will most likely die. We're definitely having a moment."

"No one dies from falling elevators anymore," she said. "Get with the times."

"Let me show you how it's done," he said. He reached for her but she held up her purse between them like a shield. "Don't be afraid," he coaxed.

"I'm not afraid, I'm repulsed. I don't want your monkey pox."

"Malaria isn't communicable," he said.

"Without Google, all I have is your word and, no offense, but your word holds no water with me."

"I'm fairly certain when you said 'no offense' you actually meant to offend me. Good thing for you I don't bruise easily and so no offense was actually taken. Now, hold still and let me kiss you proper."

"No."

"Lou, come on. How are you going to learn if I don't teach you?" he said. "I'm your best friend; it's my duty to teach you things."

"I haven't seen you in fifteen years, you jungle diseased weirdo," she said. "And I don't need you to teach me. I know how to kiss. I'm good at it, very, very good."

"Prove it," he taunted.

Lou was a lot of things, but stupid wasn't one of them. She knew exactly what he was doing. On the other hand, he was making her so angry she didn't care if she let him win. At this moment, all she wanted was to make him shut up, to prove to him she was, in fact, a good kisser. She tossed her purse aside and plunged her fingers in his hair, pulling his face close to hers. The temptation was there to kiss him now, but he was right; she was angry, and angry kisses weren't good kisses. So for a long time, she didn't do anything at all. She held his face in her hands and looked at him while he looked at her. It was an intimate, intense moment. She had no idea what she was searching for until she saw it. Eventually his look slid from amusement to confusion to something else, either concern or desire, she couldn't tell. But that was the moment she had been waiting for. So she kissed him.

She put a lot of heart and passion into that kiss, more than she had ever done before, not because she wanted him, but because she wanted so badly to beat him. But biology had its revenge and her body began to take over. A spark of desire lit in her belly and grew and grew until it threatened to consume her. This was Benny, her onetime best friend she had long ago convinced herself she was in love with.

Benny was having the same problem. What started as fun and games had turned into something more, and now both of them were wading into dangerous territory without their boots on.

He pulled her full against him and pressed her back to the wall. His lips left hers and trailed to her neck. "Lou," he whispered.

Benny, she thought, but she didn't say it out loud. Or did she? Someone did.

"Benny, hello, can you hear me?" The shout came from overhead. Benny and Lou practically fell away from each other in their haste to break apart.

"Down here," Benny tried, but his voice came out in a croaked whisper.

"We're down here," Lou shouted and she must have been heard because, next moment, the hatch at the top of the elevator opened and a firefighter was peering down at them.

"Boy, are we glad to see you," he said.

"Same here," Benny said.

"Yes," Lou added lamely.

"Secure yourselves with these. It's not too stable up here; we're going to draw y'all up." He tossed them two cables and waited to make sure they tied them properly. Lou had never been good at knots, but Benny was. He shooed her fingers aside and tied the knot around her waist. His fingers shook. She pretended not to notice.

A few minutes after that they were being pulled up, up, up—one at a time, with Benny insisting Lou go first—until a fireman standing on the floor above them caught them and pulled them back onto stable ground. Three firemen and all the Samperis were there to greet them.

"What are you guys doing here?" Lou asked, but Benny seemed to take their appearance for granted.

"Benny didn't show up for supper," a teary-eyed Mrs. Samperi said.

Lou tried to imagine anyone tracking her down for anything if she didn't show up, but the mental image wouldn't form.

The Samperis voices echoed loudly in the marble hallway, creating enough noise for five families. Lou stepped to the side so she could hear what the fireman was saying.

"A couple of cables snapped. This elevator should never have passed inspection. It's obviously been fraying for some time," he said.

Unknown to her, Benny had eased closer to eavesdrop. He sidled beside her and laid his hand on her arm. Leaning in, he spoke softly. "Here's the deal, Lou. You're going to give me the money for the trip, or I'm going to sue the pants off you."

CHAPTER 3

"You can't sue me. That elevator was inspected; I have the records to prove it," Lou said. It was two days after the elevator incident, and now it was her turn to sit in his office. Comparatively, hers won hands down. Benny's office was a glorified construction trailer while Lou's was a luxurious penthouse at the tallest and most prestigious building in town. But that was as it should be—her family business was finance while his was construction. She needed the appearance of wealth while he needed the appearance of getting things done.

Benny picked up the phone. "Molly, get me a lawyer, the one with the giant billboard by *McDonald's*." He hung up. He and Lou waited in silence a minute until the phone beeped.

"I have Rhett Mullins on line one," Molly said.

Benny pushed the button and put the lawyer on speakerphone. "Mr. Mullins, this is Benedict Samperi. I'm sure you heard about the unfortunate elevator incident at Lawton tower. I'm sitting here with Lou Lawton who is telling me I have no case against her and her company."

"I sure am glad you called me, Benedict, because you sure as shooting do have a case against Ms. Lawton. The liability compensation alone could run into six or seven figures," Rhett Mullins began before launching into a detailed plan of action to get the lawsuit ball rolling. "I have a contract right here, and I can meet with you at your earliest convenience," Rhett finally finished. His voice was as oily as a tin can of sardines.

"Thank you for your time. I'll think it over and get back to you," Benny said. He pushed the button to disconnect. He and Lou surveyed each other again.

"Why are you doing this? We handle your accounts. I know the Samperis have enough to sponsor this event, or a string of events. Is this a power thing? Do you want to win that much?" she asked.

"No. You're right; we have the money to do it ourselves. But this is a community event. Churches all over town have gathered donations, school children have donated pennies and quarters, there have been fundraisers almost nonstop since the tornado touched down. This is a *community* event, Lou, and the Lawton group is part of this community. I don't want my family's involvement to overshadow the town's involvement," he said. "And then there's the fact you already promised the money. Think of what it would do to your reputation if you reneged."

"Good guy Benny to the rescue again," she goaded, but he didn't take the bait. He waited her out, and eventually she caved. "Fine, you can have the money. Are you happy?"

"There's one more thing. I want you to come along," he said.

"No."

"Yes."

"No."

"Yes or I'm calling Rhett Mullins back," he threatened.

"Why are you doing this to me? Is it because of what happened in the elevator? Because that was no big deal."

"Yes, Lou, you caught me. We shared one kiss in two decades, and now I've decided to rearrange our lives and force you to go on a mission trip in order to pursue you," he said.

"Sarcastic point taken, but you still didn't answer my question. Why do you want me to go?"

"Because I think you need this."

"You think I need this? Who are you to say what I need? Who are you to presume to know me at all anymore?"

"Fair enough, but let me ask you a question: When was the last time you gave of yourself for someone else?" he said.

"You really should have been a priest, you know, Benny? And this goody-goody act you have going on is incredibly wearisome," she said.

"You can tell me all about it on the trip," he said.

She wanted to stomp out of the room, but having a limp and leg braces made stomping impossible. She stood. "Sometimes I really think I might hate you."

"That's not what your lips said the other night," he said, and had the audacity to add a lascivious eyebrow wag.

"How do you have everyone else fooled? I don't understand. 'Oh, Benny's such a good guy,'" she made her voice high-pitched and simpering. "I've heard it my whole life, and I'm so sick of it."

"If I remember correctly, you said it yourself once," he said.

"Yes, well, we both know how that ended, don't we?" she said.

"I'll send you a packing list," he said.

"Keep your list. I don't want anything from you," she said.

"Suit yourself," he said. He watched her walk away, her spine straight, her limp barely noticeable. Her left hand, the one that couldn't open all the way, was now fisted at her side. He waited until she was gone, and then he sat back, deflated. Would he ever get his energy back? Would he ever feel like himself again?

"Did you get the money?" His older brother, Joe, poked his head in the door.

"We got it," Benny said.

"Yes," Joe said, pumping his fist. "What'd you say to change her mind?"

"I pointed out the benefits of community involvement," Benny said.

"You could talk an armadillo into giving up its shell, if it were for charity," Joe said.

Benny gave him a half-hearted smile.

"Are you feeling okay?" Joe asked. His family had been worried about him since he returned to the states, his body wasted and half-dead, his mind and heart weary to the point of giving up. "You don't have to do this, you know. We could send someone else to head up the construction team. Any of us could do it." Except Moss who didn't have a leadership bone in his body.

"I'm fine, and I'm looking forward to it. Lou Lawton's going to come along," he said.

"Really? You guys used to be good friends before she left. Maybe you'll have a chance to reconnect on this trip," Joe said.

"I doubt it. She hates me."

"Nobody hates you," Joe said.

"Lou does," Benny said. He could see the curiosity written on his brother's face, but he had never told anyone what transpired between him and Lou and he wasn't about to start now. "How's Peaches?" he asked instead. His sister-in-law, so long a part of his life he couldn't remember a time without her, had always felt like a real sister to him.

Joe sighed and sank heavily into the chair Lou had recently vacated. "I don't know, Ben. She seems so far away. I'm not sure I know how to reach her anymore." He looked at Benny the way everyone looked at him, as if he were a magician who held the wisdom of life. But Benny had never been married; he had no answers other than the obvious.

"Peaches loves you, and you love her. Don't forget, and don't stop trying." Joe nodded, looking defeated. Benny hated seeing his unbreakable big brother so...broken. More than that, he hated feeling powerless to help. "Do you want me to talk to Peaches?" Why was he offering to do that? He didn't want to get in the middle of their mess.

"Thanks, but no. I think more Samperi involvement is the last thing she needs right now," Joe said.

"If you need anything," Benny let the offer hang, mostly because he had no idea what he could give. But, like always, he desperately wanted to help. He had learned the hard way that wanting to help and being able to help were two different things.

"I'd better get back to work. And, hey, don't let that Lou thing get you down. I'm sure she'll come around. No one can stay mad at you for long," Joe said.

That's what you think, Benny thought. Because the thing Joe didn't realize was Lou had every reason in the world to loathe him as much as she did.

CHAPTER 4

hey met in fourth grade, Benny's first day of school in
Kentucky after his family moved from Brooklyn. Unlike
with Joe and Peaches, it hadn't been an instant love match. Benny
preferred spending time with other boys and Lou had been the girl in
the wheelchair. Though they had been classmates for years, they
didn't remember each other much until middle school. That was
when Lou's mom suggested having a pool party for the class. While
Lou's legs didn't function well on land, she was like a mermaid in the
water, sleek and unstoppable. The party was supposed to be her
chance to shine, to try and connect with other kids on their level.
That had been the intent, until the boys discovered the game room in
the basement and everyone abandoned the pool. Everyone but Benedict Samperi, whose sensitivity and compassion were starting to
emerge as key character traits. He alone seemed to understand Lou's
feelings that day—her desperation to fit in, her consternation over the
plan that was now failing, and even her inability to emerge from the
pool unassisted. It had been he who rounded up the missing party-
goers and brought them back to the pool. Best of all, he did it without
exposing Lou's vulnerability. In addition to having a heart for the

hopeless, Benny had started to show a charisma that made him a natural-born leader.

From that moment on, Lou and Benny had been friends, eventually and seamlessly they became best friends. They never talked about that night, never articulated Lou's distress or Benny's rescue. But it had cemented something between them, some unspoken bond. By all rights, Lou should have adored him as her hero, but she didn't. Theirs was a sarcastic friendship, almost brutal in its honesty. She told him when he was being self-righteous and pompous and he told her when she was being caustic and self-involved. As their friendship developed, they found they had a lot in common. Both of them had been born into families where their careers were predestined. They were both expected to go into the family business—Benny to construction and Lou to finance.

It took Lou a long time to realize Benny was different with her than he was with everyone else. No one else saw his quick wit and cutting sense of humor. No one else heard the sometimes snarky asides he whispered under his breath, the ones that made her laugh so hard she often got in trouble. Everyone else seemed to think he was perfect, a constant helper with the temperament of an angel. Even his friendship with her had been a point in his favor. *Isn't Benny nice to befriend the girl in the wheelchair?*

At first she thought other people must not know him the way she did. Slowly she began to understand he didn't display himself to others the way he displayed himself to her. As they headed into high school, she began to fool herself into thinking that was because there was something special between them, more than their close friendship, and so she fell in love. She genuinely believed they could be the sort of best friends who turned their relationship into something deep and lasting, a true love that would last forever. Not only was she stupid enough to fall for him, she was naïve enough to believe he loved her in return. When he asked her to prom their junior year, her unfounded suspicions were confirmed.

Lou was not the type of girl to get excited about anything, but she had been excited about prom. She had believed it marked a turn in their relationship, from friendship to romance. And though Benny didn't display any hints of romance before the dance, she thought there had been a growing tension and awareness between them. She convinced herself he was saving his expressions of love for the big night.

Unknown to him, she had been working hard to get out of her chair. It wasn't that she couldn't walk, but cerebral palsy had left the muscles in her legs and left arm weak. She could walk down a hallway unassisted. After that, she needed support. The chair was easier, but Lou had always been goal-oriented. She set herself an objective to dance one entire dance at the prom, and worked relentlessly with her physical therapist until she was sure she could accomplish her goal.

Then the morning of the prom came and the phone rang. A few minutes later, Lou's mom entered the room, her face crestfallen. "Bad news, honey. Benny's really sick. His mom thinks maybe it's strep; she's getting ready to take him to the doctor. She said he would have called you himself, but he can't talk. Laryngitis." She didn't have to tell Lou prom was off the table because it was obvious. As much as Lou wanted to go, she didn't want to drag a sick boy there and watch him be miserable all night.

"Oh," Lou said, trying hard not to cry. She had surpassed the age where she was comfortable crying in front of her parents, or anyone, for that matter.

"I had an idea, though. Maybe you could take him a little care package. We could put together some snacks and juice, some books and magazines, and maybe a video game and take it over. Sound good?" Her mom's hopeful face was heartbreaking. She had wanted the date to go well almost as much as Lou had. Maybe more.

"Sounds good, Mom," Lou said, trying to muster enthusiasm. In reality it sounded sort of pathetic, as if she were still trying to pawn herself on Benny when he was sick. But she did want to see him, and she could always tell him the care package had been her mom's idea. If there was anyone who understood family interference, it was Benny Samperi.

Later that afternoon, after Benny returned from the doctor, Lou and her mom headed to the store and assembled a care package for him. Though she still felt mildly embarrassed about it, Lou had fun selecting items she knew he'd enjoy. They arrived unannounced at the Samperi's house, but his mom welcomed them with a smile. Their new house had recently been completed and she was anxious to show it off. The two mothers talked in the kitchen while Mrs. Samperi motioned down the hall toward Benny's room.

"I'm sure he'll be glad for the company, Lou. He's been a little bored," Mrs. Samperi said. Lou wasn't sure how it was possible to be bored in such a noisy house. Benny's younger siblings seemed to be playing some sort of cops and robbers game and were running around the living room screeching at full volume while his dad watched a game on television. The kitchen smelled like garlic and tomatoes. All in all, it was a comforting, chaotic scene.

Lou wheeled herself down the long, wide hallway and paused outside Benny's door. Taking a breath, she hitched herself out of the chair. They might not be able to dance, but she could still surprise him by walking into his room. He probably didn't realize she could walk because he had never seen her do so. The chair was so much easier and faster. Plus she was embarrassed over the way her body limped and wobbled. Somehow the chair was less embarrassing than the failed performance of her body.

She raised her hand to knock before remembering he had laryngitis and might not be able to answer. It was half open already, so she pushed it the rest of the way, stepped inside, and froze.

Benny stood in the center of the room playing video games, hopping from foot to foot and yelling—*yelling*—at the screen.

"I guess you made a miraculous recovery," she said. Her voice came out softer than she intended, but somehow he heard her.

It was possible he actually was feeling momentarily better, that medicine or rest had helped him. But when he turned to look at her, she knew. Guilt was written all over his face. He had ditched her, on prom night.

"Lou," he said. His face went white, from guilt not fever, and he reached a hand toward her.

She turned, slowly so she wouldn't fall over, sat back down in her chair, and wheeled quickly down the hallway. He didn't follow.

On Monday she wasn't at school, and she never came back again. No one ever knew why, and no one speculated much. Most people presumed she was being homeschooled because it had become too difficult to get around in her chair. That part could have been true. They went to a two-story school. Lou had to obtain a special key to use the handicapped elevator, making her late to almost every class. She had also been assigned a fulltime aid to help her get around and go to the bathroom. Most kids wondered why she had stayed so long with so many obstacles to overcome. Only Benny knew the truth. She had dropped out because of him, because he had eviscerated her heart.

CHAPTER 5

For a once predictable life, Hattie Lou Lawton's path was turning out to be anything but. She had always known she was destined to take over the family business, but she wouldn't have guessed the twisted road she would have taken to get there. She had assumed she would graduate from the local high school and go to college somewhere in Kentucky before taking over the reins of her father's company. Instead, before her senior year of high school, she transferred to a European boarding school. That change became the springboard for acceptance into an Ivy League university on the east coast. Then when she returned home, newly self-assured to the point of cockiness, she had expected to step immediately into her father's shoes. Instead he had made her start at the bottom rung as a call taker and complaint handler. The senior investors in the firm had loved ordering the boss's daughter about. "Lou, there's a box of copy paper in the basement. Go get it." "Lou, the coffee tastes bitter. Make a fresh pot."

After the initial sting of wounded pride, Lou had learned to keep her mouth shut and take orders. And she had learned a lot more than that. By talking to upset customers on the phone, she had learned how to deal with difficult people in difficult situations. And she had learned to have compassion for people in a financial panic. From those senior investors, whom she eventually realized gave the same good-natured ribbing to all new employees, she had learned valuable investment strategies, such as when to wait and hold on and when to jump ahead and take a chance.

In the end, she did take over for her father, but not until she'd put in a few years hard labor climbing the ranks. By the time she reached the top, she felt humbled by her position and ready to try and lead those below her. She was a good boss, at least in her own estimation, and she wouldn't have been if her father hadn't had the wisdom and foresight to make her begin at the beginning.

And now she was going on a mission trip. With Benedict Samperi, her former friend and present mortal enemy. Perhaps mortal enemy was a bit strong. Maybe she should call him the man who ruined her life forever, though, to be fair, he hadn't. But calling him the first man who shattered her heart was too wordy and melodramatic.

The morning of the mission trip started early, but Lou was used to early mornings. Her father's philosophy had been that the boss should be the first one to arrive and the last one to leave. Lou carried on the tradition. Despite her readiness for the early hour, she was quiet as she chose a seat on the bus and stared absently out the window. She didn't want to do this. When it came to people, she was good at the surface stuff. Schmoozing and networking were her lifeblood. But spending quality one-on-one time with strangers for days on end held no appeal. Trekking to some forsaken, poverty-stricken, tornado-ravaged backcountry ranked even lower on her list. A deal was a deal, however. Benny was waiting for her to throw in the towel and back out. She refused to give him the satisfaction.

The empty space beside her was suddenly filled with someone's presence. Lou had hoped to have the seat to herself. But as she turned to look, she saw with surprise the bus was filled to capacity.

"Hi, I'm Molly," the girl said. She was a cute girl, all doe-eyed and gentle. Her long brown hair had been swept up into a bouncy ponytail and her lips had a deep cupid's bow, giving her almost the appearance of a perpetual pucker. Lou felt immediately drawn to her, not because she was cute, but because she seemed intelligent and highly capable. Lou, who had been in charge of a company for half a decade, realized talent when she saw it. Her internal radar tuned to Molly who, if Lou was correct, hadn't yet reached or maybe even realized her full potential.

"You're the Samperis' secretary," Lou said, a little sharper than she'd intended. Was Molly a spy, sent to make sure Lou followed through with her end of the bargain?

"I am," Molly agreed, slightly taken aback by Lou's abruptness.

Lou realized, as the girl gazed at her with something like fear, that she was being paranoid. "Lou Lawton," Lou said, holding out her hand. Molly took it and shook. Meanwhile Lou reminded herself women didn't usually shake hands upon meeting.

Finance was a man's world, and Lou had become accustomed to making herself more masculine to fit in. At work, she greeted people with direct eye contact and a firm handshake. She had also learned to take qualifiers out of her vocabulary. Instead of saying, "I think maybe we should meet on Thursday, if it's okay with everyone," she now said, "We'll meet on Thursday." Language was only one of the subtle differences between the genders, one that sometimes restrained women from getting ahead in business. Lou had spent nearly a decade learning to recognize and remove those differences with surgeon-like precision. The outcome was that she thrived in the work world. The drawback was that she was sometimes viewed as too forceful and domineering in her social life.

"You must handle a lot of responsibility at your job. Being the lone secretary for such a booming company is no small task," Lou said, purposely softening her tone.

Molly's face lit. "I'm one of those people who thrives under pressure, and the Samperis are great to work for. Plus it's been a little easier since Benny came home. He's been handling a lot of the paperwork until he regains his strength. Before, Joe and Giovanni split the paperwork, but they were always out on a job, so I was forever trying to track one of them down before a deadline expired." The flow of words came to a sudden halt, as if she feared she had revealed too much private information to an outsider.

Lou found it fascinating, however. She had wondered how their division of labor worked. Their father, Pete Samperi, was largely retired and only did what he termed "fun jobs," things like driving heavy machinery and occasional finish work. With five siblings, Lou had long wondered if there was bickering over who did what or if each person played to his/her strengths. She would like to be a fly on the wall at one of their meetings sometime. Did Joe, the eldest, hand out assignments? Or did everyone already know what to do? Someone had to be in charge, to make them so cohesive. Did that person inspire resentment among the others? Lou wanted to ask, but she had the feeling Molly was done talking about her job.

The attention on the bus shifted to the front. Benny stood and, as usual, had everyone's immediate attention without trying. *He could definitely lead a cult, if he wanted,* Lou thought, and not for the first time. She tuned him out while he gave the usual spiel, thanking the assembled crew for their effort and time. Then she heard her name and her eyes snapped forward.

"Special thanks to Lou Lawton, who has not only generously sponsored this outing, but also volunteered to come along and help. Stand up, Lou." He held out his hand in her direction, inviting everyone's eyes to settle curiously on her. She shook her head, glaring daggers at Benny. "She's shy," he added while a few people chuckled.

"That was...odd," Molly observed, more to herself than to Lou. "I've never seen Benny purposely try to make anyone feel awkward and exposed before."

"Ben and I go back a long way," Lou explained.

Molly wanted to ask more questions, Lou could tell, but she wisely kept them to herself.

When he was finished with his speech, Benny turned and spoke to Molly. "Could you double check the coolers before we take off, Molly? I want to make sure we have enough ice."

"Sure," Molly said. She eased out of the seat and Benny filled it.

"I don't want to sit by you," Lou said. "You have monkey cooties. I'd prefer Molly."

"No," Benny said. "I don't want you poaching Molly."

"What's that supposed to mean?" Lou asked.

"She's the best secretary we've ever had. You have an eye for good people and a vendetta. I don't want you to take her," he said.

"The malaria has addled the deep places in your brain, George of the Jungle. Do you hear yourself? I'm not John Gotti. I don't have vendettas, and I don't poach humans," Lou said though, in fact, she had already thought about offering Molly a job, if she continued to be impressive and competent. And part of that thought was due to the fact that she wanted to stick it to the Samperis, namely Benedict.

"I know you," Ben said, giving her such a look of smug superiority she wanted to poke him in the cheek to make it go away.

"You don't know me. You knew me when I was a kid; there's a difference," she said.

"Tell me what's changed then, because the girl I knew was one of the most competitive, proud people to ever walk the planet. Is the new, grownup Hattie Lou Lawton any different?" He squeezed her knee in a tender spot that was half ticklish, half painful. She pried his fingers away and gave them a shove.

"I'm in full command of my baser instincts and emotions now," she said.

"You always were," he said. "If you want to fall asleep and rest your head on my shoulder, feel free. I'm here for you."

"I'd rather you be somewhere else for me," Lou said.

"Can't, all the seats are taken."

She glanced around and saw Molly now sitting with Moss, the youngest Samperi brother. "Are you trying to shove Molly into the path of your little brother, thereby fortifying some kind of blood alliance?"

"That's medieval and creepy. But in my vast experience, there is always a mission trip romance. Do you want to take bets on who it will be?"

She scanned the interior of the bus again. "Your other brother looks pretty cozy with his seatmate."

"Giovanni? I should hope so—that's his wife."

"There was a Samperi wedding? I really need to crawl out from beneath my rock more," Lou said.

"There was no wedding—there was a sketchy first date elopement," Benny said.

"How did your mom take that?" Lou asked.

"The promise of future grandchildren is a healing balm," Benny said.

"There, those two, that's your mission romance," Lou said. She sat on her knees and peered over the seat, using her head to indicate her targets.

Ben swiveled his head to look. The male in question, a dark-skinned boy of about eighteen, was laughing and talking with his friends. The girl, a pale brunette approximately the same age, sat with her nose buried in a boring looking textbook. "Frat boy and bookworm? Nah, too cliché," he said.

"It's every bookworm's fantasy, that the popular, handsome guy will see past the quiet façade," Lou said.

"Was that your fantasy?" he asked.

"Did you consider me a bookworm?" Lou countered. She had been neither quiet nor a devoted reader growing up.

"No, but you always maintained a hands-off vibe. There were only a few people allowed behind the veil."

She was uncomfortable with the aptness of his description. After so many years of hurt and rejection by other kids, she had learned not to open herself up to people. Benny had wormed his way behind her defenses, and look how that turned out. Besides her parents, he had been the person she loved the most in the world, and that was why the hurt had gone so deep.

"Lou, about that night," he began, his tone apologetic.

She cut him off. "Ancient history, and I don't want to talk about it."

They were silent a few beats until he spoke again. "Where did you go senior year? There were rumors."

"What kind of rumors?" she asked.

"Mostly that your dad took you out of the country for illegal medical treatments," he said.

Lou was surprised people had cared enough to make up rumors about her. "I went to Vauxhall, a Swedish boarding school."

"For what it's worth, it wasn't the same without you. Senior year was lonely and boring with no one to talk to," he said.

"Oh, please," Lou said.

"Why don't you believe me?" he said.

"You were Mr. Popular, beloved by kids and teachers alike, involved in everything, invited to every gathering of more than two people. I have a hard time picturing you crying alone on a Saturday night."

"I was busy, true, but there's nothing lonelier than being alone in a crowd," he said. "High school wasn't the same without my best friend."

Lou knew better than anyone, but she still wasn't buying his spin on things. "That sounds like a line, and a lame one."

"Would it prove my sincerity if I cried?" he asked, but he was smiling.

"Yes, because nothing says 'sincere' like a few manufactured tears," she said.

"Does the fact I've devoted the majority of my life to humanitarian work do nothing to expunge my past misdeeds, Lou?" he asked.

"No, because I still think you're a fraud."

"You believe I've fooled everyone in the world except you," he said.

"That's right," Lou said. "Now why are you smiling?"

"It's kind of nice to be thought of as the bad boy for once," he said. "Maybe I'll get a leather jacket, take a spin on a Harley."

"You could probably murder a nun in plain view of your friends and family, and they would still find a way to justify it as an act of charity," she said.

"You won't let me apologize or explain, so what do I have to do to get you to forgive me?" he asked.

"I never said I don't forgive you," she said. "The past is done, and I've moved on."

"So, we're friends," he said.

"Of course we're not friends, Tarzan. We don't know each other," she said.

"We know the fundamentals, and that's what's important," he said.

"I don't like your fundamentals," she said.

"That's not what your lips said in that elevator," he said.

"Shhh," she hushed him with a finger to her lips. "That was a heat of the moment thing, a near-death experience. And I would prefer to forget it, Curious George."

"You know a shocking amount of jungle references for someone who lives in the middle of Kentucky. And there's a lot about me you want to forget," he said. "I wonder why."

"You insisted I come on this trip, and I'm here. Let's plod through it as painlessly as possible. I'll do whatever you want me to do to get through it. When this trip is over, you can go back to saving the world, I'll go back to running my firm, and we'll pretend we've never met. Deal, Jumanji?" She held out her hand to shake.

He took her hand and kissed it. "No deal, Lou."

"Why not?" With effort, she pried her fingers from his grasp.

"Because I think you need me in your life," he said.

"Of all the big headed, egotistical statements in the world, I think that one might win the prize," she said.

"You didn't let me finish," he said. "I think you might need me in your life, and I'm almost certain I need you in mine."

CHAPTER 6

*L*ou had nothing to say after that remark. She didn't trust him, and he didn't press her on it. To be fair, she didn't trust anyone anymore, and it was only partly his fault.

They resumed the bus ride in silence. Lou checked messages on her phone while Benny studied a stack of papers she assumed was some sort of itinerary. Soon the bus turned off the highway and began winding through mountain passages so deep and narrow, Lou thought she might be ill. And when she thought it couldn't get worse, it did. It turned out the roads they had been on were highways at least halfway maintained by the state. Soon enough they turned onto county roads, some not even paved. The bus bumped roughly over dirt and gravel. Lou gripped the seat in front of her and tried not to grimace with every jolt. Her body, partially lame as it was, was not well suited to backwater travel. Beside her Benny smiled like a fool.

"You're loving this, aren't you?" she asked as the bus hit a rut so deep she nearly flopped over the seat in front of her.

"This is nothing," he said. "If you want real adventure, you should ride a double decker bus in India while it winds up the side of a mountain on a two-way street only wide enough for one car. Now *that's* rustic."

"You have a mental illness," she informed him.

"Live a little, Lou," he said, still smiling the maniac smile.

Easy for you to say, she thought. He didn't have a plastic leg brace jabbing painfully into his flesh with every bump. On the other hand, his face behind the smile was rather wan and gray. It was highly possible he was faking his enthusiasm, as he faked so much of his persona for the sake of making others believe he was Mr. Wonderful.

"On a scale of one to hand me a bucket, how much do you want to puke your brains out right now?" she asked.

He laughed, a genuine sound distinctly different from his usual politely fake chuckle. Lou had forgotten the sound of that laugh, as well as the feeling it gave her to produce it. She had been one of the only people who could truly amuse him, and she had gloried in her position. "Isn't it possible I'm sick as a dog and also having fun?" he asked.

She was spared from further comment when the bus came to an abrupt halt. Had they blown a tire? Hit a cow? But no, they had arrived at their destination.

"We're here, take a look," Benny announced, softly to her, and in a tone that said it mattered to him. Lou was confused by that until she saw where they had landed.

"We're staying here?" she asked as she surveyed the giant brick mansion outside her window.

"Different than what you imagined, huh?" he asked, amused.

"I'm beginning to understand why you enjoy mission work so much," Lou said. "But won't this be kind of odd, with the helpers all staying at a luxury B&B?"

"Believe it or not, it's kind of a necessity. This is the only place in town with full power and water, so it's become the base of operations for all the mission work that's been going on."

The owner came out to the porch to greet them. "Y'all are so welcome. My lands, come in out of this heat and have some sweet tea."

"Is she for real? Does she think we're here to film a commercial for southern tourism?" Lou asked.

Benny poked her. "You be nice."

She poked him back. "You stop touching me." He winked at her, and Lou rolled her eyes. He was the type of guy who could get away with a wink and have it be cute and borderline sexy and not at all creepy or ironic. Thinking of his allure made Lou wonder why he wasn't married or if he had a girlfriend. She had always pictured him wed to some virginal type who believed in having twelve children and educating them all at home while grinding her own wheat to bake daily bread as she wove blankets out of yak fur. Instead he was thirty two, single, and recovering from what seemed to be a near-deadly bout of malaria.

"You're scanning me like you're trying to read me, Lou," he said.

"Maybe I am," she admitted.

"I'm an open book. Ask me anything, and I'll tell you. But not now. Right now, it's go time." He picked up his pack and slung it over his shoulder before ascending to the front of the bus to lead the team in disembarking.

"Go time?" Lou said when it was her turn to file past him. "The only people who talk that way are in the middle of an audition for an action movie, Chuck Norris."

"Keep it moving, Lawton," Ben said, but he was smiling an actual smile now and not the plastic one he had been wearing. Lou stepped off the air-conditioned bus and immediately wanted to go back inside. It was a scorcher of a day, so humid her clothes felt immediately damp and her leg braces began to chafe. Lou suppressed a groan, mostly because she knew Benny was waiting for her to complain, possibly even waiting for her to fail. Well, he was bound to be disappointed. She hadn't struggled herself out of a wheelchair using only physical therapy and sheer force of will, gone on to become the CEO of her father's company, and been named one of Kentucky's 40 most influential people under 40 three times running to complain about a little heat.

"Y'all come in here," their hostess said. She opened the door to the mansion while the assembled group filed past and herded inside. There was no air conditioning, but the old manse had the sort of design that kept it fairly cool. Upstairs might be another matter, but

Lou pushed that thought away. She could stand the heat for a few days, if it came down to it.

Benny climbed up a few steps so he could be taller than everyone, but it didn't matter. Everyone naturally looked to him as their leader. All eyes were on him as he started to speak.

"For those of you who didn't come with a friend or spouse, I have your room assignments." He looked at a list and began to call out names and room numbers. Eventually the crowd dwindled away until only Benny and Lou were left. "There's only one room left, and there are two of us. What a pleasant coincidence. We can hang a sheet between us, like a temporary room divider." He held the piece of paper aloft and waved it between them.

"You have got to be joking," Lou said.

"Of course I am, but good to know where you stand on the matter of cohabitation. You'll be with Molly—she's outside sorting through the luggage."

"She's sorting the luggage by herself? Geez, Samperi, even beasts of burden get a hay break," she said.

"Molly is here as a paid assistant, not a volunteer like everyone else. Plus she's a whiz at organization. There's no one I trust more to handle the details of this trip," Benny said.

"Reliable, self-directed, excellent organizational skills, and in need of an employer who doesn't use her as a pack mule. Check, check, and check. I think Miss Molly and I are going to have a productive talk tonight."

He took a step closer. "Take my secretary, Lou, and I'll take something of yours in return."

"You want my secretary? Take her. She's seventy four and been with the company for forty years. She calls the computer a Filofax, still uses a Rolodex, and last week accidentally emailed our entire client list a virus attached to a picture of a singing cat."

"I'll take something else, something more personal." He wagged his eyebrows.

Lou put her hand to her lips. "I just threw up in my mouth a little. Is there indoor plumbing here?"

He tossed her a set of keys. "Take your smart mouth to your room and see for yourself."

She found her room on the third floor. There was no elevator, and Lou felt winded from the climb, but the first sight of her new room was worth it. It was huge, had its own bathroom and air conditioner with two queen-sized beds. Lou had the suspicion it was the best room the hotel had to offer and Benny gave it to her because she was funding the trip. She didn't want or need special treatment, but she also wasn't going to complain when she received it. Besides, she would be sharing the room with Molly. True special treatment would have been letting her stay on her own, as she secretly wanted to do. She hadn't had a roommate since college and, even then, it had taken her a long time to be comfortable enough to let another person see her leg braces. Molly seemed like a sweet girl, however, and Lou felt a natural affinity for her. In Molly, Lou sensed a hidden ambition, as if she could set the world on fire if she had someone to give her the matches.

"Call me the little match girl," Lou mumbled to herself as Molly opened the door and began dragging in suitcases.

"I would have helped you carry those," Lou said. It would have cost her a lot of energy and soreness, but she would have done it nonetheless.

"It's no problem," Molly said, panting slightly from exertion. Lou hadn't packed especially lightly and the poor girl had struggled all of her suitcases up three flights of stairs.

"Here, let me take those," Lou said. She reached around Molly and began dragging bags into the room. "I don't usually pack this much, I promise. But I wasn't sure what to expect."

"Didn't Benny give you a packing list?" Molly said.

"He tried," Lou admitted. "I sort of told him to shove it where the sun don't shine."

Molly chuckled uncomfortably. "I've never met anyone who didn't like Benny before."

"I used to like Benny a whole lot. He was my best friend from middle through high school," Lou said and left it at that.

Molly was dying to know what happened; Lou could read it on her face. To her credit, she kept her questions to herself and went about arranging her things in her half of the room.

"Do you like working for the Samperis?" Lou asked.

"I love it. They're like family," Molly said.

"They're not, though," Lou said and then, seeing Molly's expression, added, "I'm sorry, I'm kind of abrupt and lacking a softening filter sometimes, or always. The Samperis are good people, but they're still your employers. Forgetting that would be a professional mistake. Business is business. At the end of the day, they sign your check and that's all."

Molly offered up a tentative smile. "Benny warned me you might try to poach me."

"Malaria has made him paranoid. If I were trying to poach you, you'd know it by my generous incentive package. This is me offering some free advice, one business woman to another. It's a tough world out there, and we have to take care of each other." Lou sat and propped her aching legs on a footstool. "What's on our agenda today? Healing the sick? Ministering to the poor and downtrodden? Turning water into wine?"

Molly pulled out her itinerary. "It says we're supposed to settle in while Benny meets with the medical resident who will be assisting us. Then we'll tour the damage site and get a feel for the projects we'll be working on. The real work starts tomorrow."

"It actually says 'the real work starts tomorrow' doesn't it?" Lou asked.

"How did you know?" Molly asked.

"The corniness has Ben written all over it," Lou said. "Can I see?" She held out her hand. Reluctantly, Molly turned over her printout of the week's activities. It was going to be a jam-packed seven days with multiple projects taking place and Benny in charge of all of it. He had himself scheduled to be in several places at once and, knowing him, he would somehow do it. Lou refrained from rolling her eyes, but she wanted to. "St. Benedict is going to kill himself."

"He says he likes to be busy," Molly said.

Lou knew he liked to be needed and important, a savior to all the unwashed masses. But there was no need to enlighten Molly when the girl probably wouldn't believe her anyway. People saw what they wanted to see in Benny. "Does this place have a pool?"

"It does," Molly said, blinking at the abrupt change in topic.

"Do I have time for a swim?" Lou asked.

"Definitely," Molly said. "We have a generous hour before we have to go anywhere."

"Great. Do you want to come?"

"No, thanks. I have some stuff to do for Benny before he gets back," Molly said.

"Make sure he's paying you for the overtime. Benny has a way of making people work for free," Lou said.

"I'm glad to help," Molly said.

"Molly, Molly, Molly, you've already been infected," Lou said. "Let me negotiate your salary for you and you'll be driving a Bentley by this time next year."

Molly laughed. "I'll keep that in mind."

Lou changed into her bathing suit and full-length robe. She would wait until she was by the pool to take off her braces, mostly because she wouldn't be able to navigate the stairs well without them, but also because she didn't want people to stare. The pool would feel heavenly on such a muggy day, but for Lou it was more a necessity than luxury. Swimming kept her muscles limber and gave her legs a break from the unceasing structure of the braces. With so much walking and climbing and standing coming up in the next few days, she would need all the swim breaks she could get.

CHAPTER 7

No one was near the pool, and Lou breathed a sigh of relief as she sat and began unfastening her braces. It would be a wobbly walk to the pool, but it was only a few steps. She reached the pool safely and slipped into the cool water with something akin to delight. The only time her body felt truly free and fully in her control was when she swam. Then her legs did exactly what she asked them to with no rebellious wobble. Her arms cut through the water as if they had all the strength and grace in the world, regardless of the fact that her left hand was perpetually drawn into itself.

She swam for what felt like a long time, until she knew it had to be time to get out and get ready. When she finally surfaced, Benny sat at the water's edge, her robe in his lap.

"That's private property," Lou said. She wanted him to go away. She didn't want him to see her weak attempts to get out of the pool. Getting out was the worst part. At home she had a special rail and a ramp to help. Here she would have to struggle like a suffocating catfish, and she would have to do it in front of Benedict Samperi.

"I like to watch you swim," Benny said.

"Lone Creeper, party of one, your table is ready," Lou said.

"You're graceful. It's sort of soothing to watch you glide back and forth with hardly a ripple. I can feel my blood pressure sinking," he said.

"A fish tank would be a more socially acceptable hobby than a people tank," she informed him. She swam to the side and clung to the edge. "Are you going to leave soon?"

"No. Here." He put his hands down to help her out. Drat him for discovering her secret worry. She wanted to refuse his help, but was chagrined to realize how much she needed it. She gave him her hands and he lifted her out with ease, wrapping her in her robe.

Lou sat and reached for her braces. "I don't suppose you're going to go away now, are you?"

"Nope." He sat on the chair across from her and watched while she reattached her braces.

"Why are you smiling like that?" she asked.

"Because you have nice legs and I'm betting not a lot of people get to see them. So it's sort of a privilege."

"Did you want something or are you prepping for your stalking trial, should I ever get enough evidence to convict you?" Lou said.

"I need a favor," he said.

"The first step is identifying the problem. Good luck finding a solution," Lou said. She stood to go.

Benny stood so they were toe to toe. "I need a favor from you, o reigning queen of sarcasm."

"For laughs, let's hear what it is," Lou said.

"I met with the medical resident," he said.

"Let me guess—she said you have malaria. Kids are so bright these days," Lou said.

"She is bright and eager, a very attractive young woman," he said.

"When's the wedding?" Lou asked.

"That's the problem. See, a lot of times in these situations, women sort of…" he trailed off, searching for the best way to say it.

"Are you trying to tell me women can't stop falling in love with you wherever you go?" she said.

He nodded.

"You poor, miserable man. Bless your heart. I'm going to go alert the Red Cross, see if they can arrange some sort of fundraiser for you," Lou said. She tried to get by him, but he put his hands on her shoulders.

"I know how this sounds, especially to you. Usually it's not that big of a deal and I sort of try to brush it off. But I'm using every last ounce of energy I have to function through the malaria right now, and I can't handle one more thing. So I'm asking if you would consider sort of posing as my love interest for the week."

Lou put her hands over her face and laughed. "Are you seriously asking me to be your pretend missionary camp girlfriend?"

"I wouldn't put it like that," Ben said.

"How would you put it?" she asked.

"This isn't a big deal. I had a friend on my mission council in Suriname who did the same thing a couple of times. She sort of ran interference for me with a few women," he said.

She dropped her hands and regarded him, searching his face. "And?"

"And what?" he said, dropping his eyes uncomfortably.

"And what happened with your friend who ran interference?" she prodded.

He sighed. "She fell in love with me. It got awkward."

Lou laughed, and he smiled. "You're unbelievable, you know that, Samperi?"

He smiled, a little self-deprecating grin. "See, Lou, this is why I need you. You're immune to me."

"That's because I've kept current on my Benedict Samperi vaccinations," she said.

He laughed and gave her shoulders a little shake. "Please, Lou, please do this for me. I don't want to hurt this girl, and I don't have the energy to outrun her this week. Plus I really need her services. There are a lot of sick people in this community who need a doctor."

Lou regarded him critically. "What's in it for me?"

He blinked, surprised. "What do you mean?"

"I know you view yourself as the puppet master of the universe, able to bend everyone to your will with merely the power of your words, Jim Jones, but I am not one of your minions. So I want something in return for doing this ridiculous favor for you."

"You can't have Molly," he said.

"Molly is a human being. I wouldn't presume to trade her like a baseball card," Lou said.

"What do you want?" he asked.

"Rumor has it your family is getting ready to launch your own show on the home and garden channel," she said.

"That's top secret information, so of course everyone knows," he said.

"I want to handle the financials for you and everyone in your family," she said.

"You can do mine, but I can't control my brothers and sister," he said.

"You can and we both know it," she said.

"Fine, you can handle all the financials," he said. "Do we have a deal?"

"There's one more thing, something more personal," she said.

"What's that?" he asked, wary now.

"I need a date for a gala in a couple of weeks. I was planning to go with my dad, but he's going to be out of town and I don't want the hassle of scoring an actual date."

"Is there anything else, your majesty?" he asked.

"That'll do for now, but if anything else comes to mind I'll let you know," she said.

"I have no doubts you will." He held out his hand, his last finger dangling in the air. "Pinky swear you'll be my fake girlfriend."

"You are twelve," she accused.

"I have a childlike enthusiasm for life," he said.

She grasped his pinky with hers and they shook on it.

"Sealing it with a kiss would probably be more appropriate," he said, inching closer.

"I'm dripping wet, smell like chlorine, and don't like you. But, sure, let's smooch," she said.

Smiling, he picked her up and gave her a squeeze. "I've missed your snark, Hattie Lou Lawton."

"And I've missed your…Give me a few months and I'll think of something," she said.

"Your first order of business as my girlfriend is to get yourself ready. We're all waiting on you to leave," he said as he set her down.

"You should realize if you attempt to order me again, I will take so long to get ready you won't leave this hotel until doomsday," she said.

"I can already tell this week is going to go exactly how I planned," he said. "Will you pretty please get ready so we may go start helping others and do what we came here to do?"

"Since you asked so nicely, yes," she said. She cinched up her robe and turned to go. He swatted her backside.

"That was for calling me Jim Jones. I'm much more David Koresh."

"You have problems, and I see them, even if others can't or won't," she said.

He kissed his fingers and waved them at her. "Save the sweet talk for later, pumpkin."

Despite her threat, Lou readied herself as quickly as she could. The thought of making anyone wait on her was enough to make her neck break out in hives. When she descended the stairs, Benny stood talking to a pretty woman with long dark hair. But when his eyes swung in her direction, they lit with a welcoming signal that hastened her over. To the outside observer it might look like he was engrossed in his conversation; to Lou, it looked like he was waiting on a rescue.

"There you are," he said. His arm reached out and slid around her, drawing her close. She allowed her hand to rest gently on his chest as she turned to the woman with a smile.

"Honey, this is Analise Diaz," Benny continued. "She's the medical resident I told you about. Analise, this is Lou Lawton."

"It's so nice to meet you," Lou said. "Benny told me how thrilled he is to have you along for the week."

"Oh, thank you," Analise said. Her eyes slid confusedly between Lou and Benny, at last settling on Lou's empty ring finger. Lou could almost see her mental wheels churning. Should she let Ben go or strengthen her resolve and pursue him despite Lou's presence? When she smiled and locked eyes on Benny, Lou knew she had made her decision. "I'm thrilled to be here with him."

Oh, no she didn't, Lou thought. She might only be a pretend girlfriend, but Analise didn't know that. Lou didn't like poachers, and especially not when it was another woman poaching on her (pretend) territory.

"We're all thrilled to be here with him," Lou agreed, gazing up at Benny with what she hoped was an appropriately adoring expression. "It will be fun to watch the master work."

Now it was Benny's turn to be confused. Of course he would have missed the undercurrent that passed between the two women. "I'm glad for any and all help," he said.

"Shouldn't we be leaving?" Lou said. "According to Molly's itinerary, we're five minutes late."

He jumped to attention. "Right, you're right, thanks. Everybody back on the bus," he called over her head. "Load up, it's time to go." He laced his fingers with Lou's and began herding her toward the bus as everyone began to file in that direction. They boarded the bus and he did a quick headcount before telling the driver they were ready to go. When the bus began to lurch forward, he slid into the seat beside Lou.

"Whew, I'm glad that's over. Thanks, Lou." He patted her leg.

"I need another shower after that performance. 'It will be fun to watch the master work,'" she imitated herself in a fawning singsong. "I've never said anything like that before in my life. Gag."

"I rather enjoyed it," Benny said.

"Of course you did. If there had been a ring full of mud we would have been in there duking it out over you," Lou said. She shuddered. "I feel unclean and ten IQ points dumber."

"Well, you can probably relax now. I think she got the point," Benny said.

Lou barked a laugh. "You are clueless, Samperi. I'm beginning to understand why these women get hooked on you; it's because you lead them on."

"I do not," he argued, affronted.

"Do you tell them straight up you're not interested?" she asked.

"No, but I don't do anything to further their crushes," he said.

"Do you cut off all communication? Do you ignore them?" she prodded.

"No because I'm not heartless. I'm polite and that's it."

"So when you know a woman has a thing for you, you continue to talk to her and treat her with your attentive brand of *kindness*," she said. "The sort where you compliment, flirt, and make a woman feel like the center of your universe."

"You're twisting everything around. You're making it sound like I want these women to fall for me as some sort of ego boost, like I try to keep them hooked for my own gratification," he said.

She raised her eyebrows at him. "Explain to me how that's not what you do. Tell me how you're direct and upfront with a woman, cutting off any expectations she might have of you. Enlighten me as to how you bar yourself from spending intimate, one on one time with them so they don't get the wrong idea."

"I don't..." he started and then stopped, frowning. "Do I?"

"You left a trail of broken hearts in high school, too, and every one of those girls genuinely believed she had a shot with you."

He sat back, deflated. "How can you be nice to a woman without leading her on?"

"Sometimes you can't be nice. Not everyone has to love you."

"Not everyone does," he said with a poke to her thigh.

"I can't be the one woman in the entire universe who doesn't adore you," she said. "What about your sister?"

"I'm the one brother she's never butted heads with," Benny informed her sadly, as if it were a burden to be so loved.

"No wonder," Lou said.

"No wonder what?" he asked.

"No wonder you're a cocky, self-righteous prig," she said.

"I am not a prig," he defended. "Prigs are no fun. I'm tons of fun. We used to have tons of fun together, Lou, admit it."

"We were children. I don't think we'd have fun together in the real world. We're too different."

"We're going to have fun this week," he declared.

"We're here to help a tornado ravaged community," she pointed out.

"No one said we can't have fun while helping others," he said.

"I don't want to have fun. I want to finish this week and get back to my real life," she said.

"Why?"

"What do you mean why?"

"What's so great about your real life?" he asked.

"I like my life," she said. "Don't you?"

"I used to. Now it's sort of up in the air." He glanced away from her, his eyes filled with a mix of sadness and a little fear.

"Drat you, Benedict Samperi, don't you go getting real on me," she said.

"I'm fine," he assured her. "A little tired."

She surprised them both by touching her fingers lightly to his cheek. "You're the same person here you are in a third-world country. Because you're not there anymore doesn't mean you're not you anymore."

"You're presuming I know who I am," he said. He tried to smile, but it didn't reach his eyes.

Her thumb smoothed over his lips as they stared at each other. The tall bus seat around them created a cocoon of privacy. "You might be a total mess, but thank the Lord you're pretty," she said.

"Good pep talk, Lou. I can always count on you for a boost."

"You can always count on me to keep it honest," she said. "And, for the record, you've spent your whole life getting boosts. Maybe what you need to do now is wallow for a bit."

"I don't believe in wallowing," Benny said.

"And therein lies your problem, Superman."

"We're here," the driver announced. The bus came to a chugging halt, and the intimate moment was over.

CHAPTER 8

The town was gone. Lou had seen it on the news, but nothing could have prepared her for the reality. There was nothing left but a few piles of rubble. Bricks were strewn haphazardly throughout the streets, along with broken two by fours mixed with pieces of tree limbs and roof shingles. Their group fell silent as the weight of what lie before them began to dawn. Two people had died in the tornado. That number had seemed like a statistic, but now it became reality. People had lived in these homes, worked and gone to school in these buildings. And now it had all been laid bare. For Lou, it was the worst devastation she had ever seen. For Benny, it wasn't even a drop in the bucket. In short order, he had rallied everyone's spirits with a pep talk.

"It may appear there is nothing left here, but that's not true. There's still a town, it simply needs to be rebuilt. There are still people who love and care about each other. They have food and running water and temporary shelter. And this week they have us."

Everyone cheered, except Lou who shook her head. The man's talent for bringing people together and inspiring them was nothing short of miraculous. He was much too charming and charismatic for his own good.

"Tonight we're going to unload the food and water we brought. The semi we sent arrived about an hour ago, I'm told. After that we'll be serving at the soup kitchen. As you can imagine, it's feeding almost the entire community right now. After cleanup, it's lights out and then we start construction bright and early tomorrow. Who's ready?"

Everyone cheered again and they set off down the street to a church, the lone building in town spared by the storm. The town's population had set up camp in FEMA trailers on the far side of the rubble. The church now functioned as a community center, meeting place, and feed hall. The group formed a line outside the church and began unloading the supplies their town had collected. Lou felt a little emotional when she saw all her hometown had lovingly gathered. There was enough food and water to last the next couple of months at least, along with a mound of toiletries and some toys for the kids.

Lou, whose arm strength wasn't great on the best of days, tried to aim for light loads, such as paper towels. But the paper towels soon ran out and she was faced with either standing by while other people worked or doing the work herself. She couldn't bring herself to stand around and do nothing, so she kept on until everything hurt and she felt like she might fall over.

A gentle hand landed on her lower back. "How are you holding up, Lawton?" Benny whispered.

"Fine," Lou lied. She caught sight of his ashen, sweaty face.

"How are you holding up, Samperi?" she asked.

"Fine," he said.

"We have that in common; we're both fine," Lou said.

"Totally and completely," Benny said. "Not about to fall over at all."

"Not even a little," Lou said, placing her hand on the side of the semi to steady herself. Benny did the same. For a minute, they stayed that way, resting and taking comfort in each other's misery.

"Well, back to being fine," Benny said and edged away.

Lou returned to her task as well. When the truck was unloaded, they served supper to the community and cleaned up. Lou spent most of her evening in the back portion of the kitchen, so she didn't have a chance to meet the community. But that was all right by her. She felt too drained and exhausted for much more.

The group tumbled onto the bus, fatigued and spent. Benny thanked them all for their service and slumped into the seat beside Lou. "You know what this reminds me of?" he said.

"The fifth circle of hell?" she guessed. The day's heat hadn't relented with the approach of nighttime. If anything, it felt more oppressive. Not even the cool air of the bus could ease Lou's sticky tiredness.

"High school," he said.

"Same difference," Lou said.

"Do you remember how we would sit together on the bus?" he asked.

"I never rode the bus; my mom drove me," she reminded him.

"I'm talking about when we went on field trips. And everyone would tease us about being a couple."

"In retrospect, we shouldn't have worn those matching 'I'm With Stupid' t-shirts," she said.

"I remember one time you got so mad and said, 'We're just friends, you hapless yokels,' and that shut them up."

"Because no one knew what a yokel was," she said. "They spent the rest of the ride trying to figure out how deeply they'd been insulted."

"Why did it make you so mad?" he asked.

"Because you never got mad. I had to get mad for the both of us," she said.

"I kind of liked it," he confessed.

"Which part?" she asked. "The sitting together, the teasing, or me being angry?"

"All of it," he said. "I never had more fun at school than when I was with you, and I kind of liked it that people thought we were a couple, and I definitely liked it when you got riled on my behalf."

"You said 'riled'. That's a cornpone word, Brooklyn," she said.

"No one has called me Brooklyn in years. I tell everyone I'm from Kentucky. Only people who really know me know about Brooklyn," he paused. "I missed home."

"Why do you say that like it's shameful? I was gone for five years, and I missed home like crazy. I missed my parents, my house, my town, my people."

"I always envisioned myself as a brazen globetrotter. For a while it was fun, but then I would be in some of the most amazing, beautiful places on the planet, and all I could think about was getting back to Kentucky."

"And now?" she asked.

"I'm enjoying being home," he said.

"But…"

"But eventually I'm going to leave again."

"Why?" she asked.

"Why? What do you mean why? It's what I do," he said. "I go where I'm needed."

"What if you're needed here?" she said.

"It's not the same," he said.

"Why not?"

"It's just not," he said, sounding uncharacteristically frustrated.

"You want to know what I think?"

"Please tell me, Lou, pretty please inform me of your opinion," he said. "It's so rare to get to hear you speak your mind."

"You have a savior complex. You want to be Superman. But you forget Clark Kent had a job, too, and it was important."

"Who in his right mind would choose to be Clark Kent over Superman?" he asked.

"Anyone who doesn't want to end up alone. Clark Kent was a son. Clark Kent was Lois Lane's boyfriend. No one dates Superman."

"What are we even talking about?" he asked. He rubbed his temples and yawned.

"We were discussing your glaring deficiencies," she said.

"How come we never discuss your deficiencies?" he asked.

"Because mine are all physical and it's impolite to make fun of the handicapped," she said.

He barked a laugh. "I have never once in twenty three years of knowing you considered you handicapped."

"Never?" she challenged.

"Never. I take that back. Does emotionally handicapped count? Because you seem terrified of intimacy."

"Says the man who flees the country to avoid relationships," she said. "Tell me the truth: did you or did you not contract malaria to get out of having a talk about your feelings with one of your devoted female followers?"

He leaned forward and pressed his lips to hers. She leaned back against the window. "What are you doing?" she asked.

"Shutting you up," he said and kissed her again.

Her arms slid around his neck and pulled him closer. "This does not mean I like you," she murmured against his lips.

"I feel ambivalent toward you, too," he said.

Beside them, someone cleared her throat. Startled, they looked up to see Molly looming over them. "Sorry," she said. "But we'll be back at the hotel in a minute, and you said you wanted to do announcements before everybody went their separate ways."

"Yes, thank you, Molly," Benny said. He sat up and ran a hand through his hair. Lou could only guess what she looked like, but Molly returned sedately to her seat without another word. Benny stood, turned to face the rest of the bus, and made his announcements while Lou stared out the window and tried to get her head on straight. What was she doing, allowing him to kiss her like that? Under no circumstances would she spark a fling with Benedict Samperi. Unless that wasn't what he had been doing. Maybe he was playing his part in the little act they had going on. Yes, that must have been it. They were both role playing and doing it well. They were supposed to be a couple so Analise wouldn't chase him. Though, if earlier today was any indication, she planned to chase him regardless.

They arrived back at the bed and breakfast. Benny allowed everyone else to disembark the bus before him and, by extension, Lou. He held out his hand to her. She frowned at it.

"I'm not one of your girls," she said.

"What?" he asked.

"I'm not one of the fawning females who will fall in love with you, no matter how good of a kisser you are," she said.

"Did it ever occur to you I want to hold your hand because I'm exhausted and it will keep me from falling over? Not everything is a diabolical plot to get to you, Lou."

"Fine," she said and put her hand in his. It was harder to stand than it should have been and she found she was glad for his assistance when he used their joined hands to help pull her up.

He kept her hand as they got off the bus and walked slowly to the inn in comfortable silence. He paused before they reached the door. "I kind of wish we could sit out here awhile and enjoy the peaceful night."

"Why don't we? There are plenty of chairs," Lou said.

He shook his head. "I'm in charge. I have to go do my part and mingle."

"Poor Benny," she said and meant it. "So bound to duty and the opinions of others."

"Poor Lou, so bound to the hurts of the past she can't open up and trust again," he said.

She bristled. "You think you're the reason I'm shut down? Don't flatter yourself, Samperi. I've been hurt and betrayed by better men than you."

"Do you want to talk about it?" His hands slid to her hips.

"No." She rested her hands on his chest.

"You said I'm a good kisser," he reminded her.

"I speak the truth, even when it's painful," she said.

"If you want honesty, how about this? I wasn't even trying before. I was phoning it in because I was tired."

"You're only saying that so I'll say prove it," she said.

"Oh, honey, you know me so well," he said. One hand moved to her neck. His thumb caressed her earlobe, and she felt herself melt a little.

"Benny."

"Hmm."

"Prove it," she whispered, and he did.

CHAPTER 9

The door to the inn opened. Benny's youngest brother, Mossimo, stood on the other side.

"I told you to have her back an hour ago. You are in big trouble, young man," he said.

"Lou, not sure if you remember my youngest brother, Moss. Moss, this is Lou."

"I remember Lou," Moss said. "You used to let me go for rides in your chair. What happened to that chair? Was it only a prop to get better parking?"

"You caught me," Lou said. "I was only recently released from prison for handicap placard fraud."

"You're funny," Moss declared. "Want to know something else? I've walked in on everyone in my family kissing someone, except Benny. I had honestly given up on him. So this was kind of a big deal."

"Now you can finish filling in that weird bingo card you've been holding onto," Lou said.

Moss laughed again and then sobered. "Hey, what's going on with you guys? Are you, like, a thing now?"

"Maybe we always were and you never realized," Benny said. He patted Moss on the shoulder and followed Lou inside. Their hostess,

Sheila, had left cookies and juice out and the gathering had assumed a party atmosphere. True to his word, Benny began to mingle. Lou let go of his hand and shooed him away. She had no desire to talk to people for the sake of making small talk with them. She found herself standing next to Benny's other brother, Giovanni, and his wife.

"You're the new Samperi," Lou said. "I'm Lou Lawton."

"I'm Vivian," the woman said, smiling sweetly. She was a good few inches shorter than Lou and had the natural sort of soft femininity Lou had always aspired to but never attained. She looked like the type of woman Lou had always imagined for Benny.

"Let me guess; you're into books," Lou said.

"I'm a librarian, but how could you possibly know that?" Vivian asked.

"Because Giovanni was the only dedicated Samperi reader. I once saw him walk into a wall while reading a Hardy Boys mystery," Lou said. She gave Giovanni's bicep a gentle squeeze.

"Spoiler alert—the smugglers did it," Giovanni said. "How have you been, Lou? You used to be a regular at the homestead, but it's been ages."

"Life has a way of going by quickly, Giovanni. Congratulations to you two, by the way. Marriage looks good on you."

"It's a good color for everyone," Giovanni said, with a significant look toward Benny.

"There's that Samperi subtlety I've missed," Lou said. "Sometimes in the night I wake up and swear I can still hear your mom yelling at Benny to leave his bedroom door open so no hanky-panky goes on."

"She still says that to us," Vivian said, and Lou laughed.

"What's funny?" Moss asked as he joined their group.

"Your face," Giovanni said.

"Ha, ha, brother humor never gets old," Moss said. "Vivian, control your man."

Molly approached their group and held out a cookie to Moss. "These are going quickly, so I scored one for you."

"Uh, thanks, I guess. I'm going to go grab some juice to go with it," Moss said and practically darted away.

"How does a cookie make him run away? I was only being polite," Molly said.

"Ignore him. He runs away from everything," Giovanni said. "I once saw him run from a gumball machine that made a loud noise, and that was only last week."

Molly laughed, but her eyes looked sad. Her gaze slid across the room and morphed into a frown. "The doctor is back. Something about her rubs me the wrong way."

"Maybe because she could only be more obvious in her attempts to bag Benny if she were wearing a hunting vest and rifle," Vivian said.

Moss sidled back to the group. "Lou, you have competition at twelve o'clock."

"That's three o'clock, dope on a rope," Giovanni said.

"It's supposed to look like an actual clock? I thought that was just something people said. It makes so much more sense now," Moss said.

"I think I'm going to go to bed," Lou said, stifling a yawn.

"You're not going to go claim your man from the competition?" Moss said.

"It's only a competition if you're afraid of losing, Moss," Lou said. She headed for the stairs. At the base, she turned to see if Benny was watching. He was. She tossed him a kiss and mouthed, *"Night."* He tossed her a kiss in return, along with a wink. She didn't spare the doctor a glance.

Later, when she lay in bed half asleep, Molly slipped in, finished up in the bathroom, and climbed into her bed.

"Lou," she whispered. "Can I ask your advice on something?"

Lou perked up and blinked sleepily. "Sure."

"How do you make a man fall in love with you?"

Lou sat up. "Molly, I have a business degree from one of the most prestigious Ivy League schools in the world. I run a multi-million dollar company with more than a hundred employees. And you want to ask me about boys?"

"Yes," Molly said.

Lou lay back down. "I have no idea. You're definitely barking up the wrong tree. Men are a mystery."

"You have Benny's interest," Molly pointed out.

"That's different," Lou said.

"How?"

Because it's not real. "We go back a long way. There's history between us. Try Vivian. She did a good job with Giovanni."

"I already asked her. She said to buy some pot brownies, but I'm pretty sure she was joking."

Lou snickered. "One thing about the Samperis, they're never boring."

"No. Kind of maddening, but never boring," Molly said. Lou didn't comment, but she couldn't have agreed more.

❦

The next morning, bright and early, Lou opened the door to see Benny standing on the other side, smiling.

"Hey, pretty girl, I'm here to walk you to breakfast."

Lou turned into the room and spoke. "See, Molly, he does like you."

"Ha, ha, hilarious. Are you coming with us, Molly?" Benny called.

"I'm not quite ready yet. You all go on without me," Molly said.

Benny's eyes swept Lou up and down. "Is that what you're wearing?"

"Is this one of those guy things where you compliment me in one breath and cut me down in the other to keep me insecure?" she asked.

"No, you look amazing, and that's the problem. You look like you're ready for a hard day at the polo club."

Lou glanced down. She was wearing flowing linen pants and a button down white cotton blouse. "I work in an office, not a car wash. I don't exactly have a lot of cut-off t-shirts and Daisy Duke shorts in my wardrobe. But these fabrics are breathable and weather appropriate."

"You're going to get filthy," he said.

"No, no, no, I'm planning to supervise while the rest of you plebes swing the hammers," she said. Then, noting his expression, rolled her eyes. "I'm joking, Samperi. Lighten up. I fully plan to get down and dirty today."

He smiled. "Yeah? We have a few minutes before breakfast. You want to start now?"

"You kiss your mother with that mouth?" she said.

"No, I kissed you."

"Don't expect a repeat. My defenses were down last night and you took advantage of my weakness," she said.

"What's that?" he asked, pointing to her hand.

"It's a baseball cap, to keep the sun off my face." She stuck it on her head and pulled her ponytail through.

"Why is your company logo on a baseball cap?" he asked.

"Because we sponsored a little league team," she said.

"Really? Did you help out?"

"I was their coach. We went all the way to state. They're making a movie about it," she said.

"Really?" he exclaimed.

She gave him a look. "I can't run or hold a bat, and I have no idea how to play baseball. Don't be gullible, Samperi."

"It's hard to reconcile such beautiful lips with such ugly lies."

She laughed, and he smiled and took her hand, the left one that didn't open completely. She tried to tug it away, but he opened her palm and kissed it. "That's for later, to remember me by," he said.

"Are you packing off to 'Nam?" she asked. "Because I have the feeling we'll see each other throughout the day."

"Yes, but this is our secret," he said.

"Definitely. Today I'm going to stare at my palm and think, 'This morning a guy with monkey pox slobbered on me.' That reminds me, I need to grab my sanitizer before we leave."

"You're not acting very girlfriendy," he accused.

She glanced around the empty hallway. "No one's here."

"If you don't practice when we're alone, you're going to forget when we're being observed," he said.

"You're right," she said. She paused and took a breath. "Where is this relationship going? Because I'm on a three year baby track, and I need a commitment." She tapped her ring finger. "Also, no more going out with your friends. You're going to be with me every night, or we're finished. How was that? Girlfriendy enough?"

"It's a good thing for you I know there's a soft, mushy center under that hard candy shell," Benny said.

"Was that supposed to be romantic? Because it kind of sounds like you want to bust me open and chew on my innards," Lou said.

He laughed, or rather guffawed. "How have you survived this long, Lou, when the list of people who want to push you into oncoming traffic must be endless?"

"I'm disabled," she said in a pathetic whimper, pointing to her legs and the braces that were covered by her long pants.

"You're a beautiful woman who would eviscerate anyone stupid enough to get in her way, who also happens to have mild cerebral palsy," he said.

"I think I found my new business card," she said, and he laughed again.

They entered the breakfast room and conversation came to a standstill as everyone paused to look at them. Lou didn't flatter herself the attention was for her. They had been waiting for Benny.

"Good morning, everyone. Who's ready to get started today?" he asked, and a general cheer went up.

"When does everyone line up for the Kool-Aid?" Lou whispered. He put her in a headlock and kissed her cheek.

"Shut it, and eat a lot because you're going to need the calories today," he said. They separated to fill their plates and sat at a table with Vivian, Giovanni, and Moss.

"I don't want to talk about it anymore," Moss was saying.

"I'm not saying you have to love her, but you have to be nice to her," Giovanni said.

"I am nice to her," Moss said.

"You flee the room every time she gets near," Giovanni argued.

"I don't want to give her the wrong idea," Moss said.

"Hear that, Benny? Moss doesn't want to give her the wrong idea," Lou said.

"You really want me to take relationship advice from Moss?" Benny said.

"Why is this anyone else's business?" Moss said. "It's between me and Molly."

"For the record, I agree with you," Lou said.

"Thank you, Lou," Moss said. He edged his chair closer to her.

"The more you alienate her and push her away, the sooner she'll be ready to come to my company," Lou continued.

Moss frowned. "What?"

"Lou has it in her head she wants to hire Molly out from under us," Benny said.

"You can't have Molly," Moss said.

"Why not? It sounds like it would be kind of a relief for you," Lou said. She picked up a piece of buttered toast and took a bite.

"She's the best secretary we ever had," Moss said.

"Secretaries are a dime a dozen. I have ten in my company; I'll give you two in exchange for one Molly," Lou said.

"You can't do that," Moss said. He turned to Benny, "Tell her she can't do that."

"Lou's not so much into the word 'can't'," Benny said, amused. "Besides, maybe she's right. Maybe we should consider letting Molly go. She clearly makes you uncomfortable, and you're a bigger part of the company than she is."

"No, I'm not…you can't take Molly. She's a good worker, and…I'm not uncomfortable around her. I don't want to hurt her, is all," Moss said.

"Then you should stop running from her and tell her straight up you're not interested. She's a grown woman, capable of handling rejection, if it's done with sincerity and truth," Lou said.

"I guess," Moss mumbled. "I'll see you guys later, I have some stuff to do."

"Tell Mom we said hi," Giovanni said.

Moss pulled out his phone and shuffled off.

"Is he really going to call your mom?" Lou asked.

"Nah, Mom's probably already parked outside with one of those parabolic listening devices," Giovanni said. "Love you, Ma." He turned to wave out the window.

"Do you think we were too hard on him?" Vivian asked.

"It was probably my fault, sorry," Lou said. She waved her hand in front of her face. "No filter."

"Are you kidding? That was awesome," Giovanni said. "Moss is like one of those balloons you punch and punch and it keeps popping back up. But I think you might actually have gotten through to him. Tell her, Benny."

"It's true. Moss has needed a dose of tough love for a while now. He tuned us out years ago," Benny said. He rested his hand on her thigh and gave it a squeeze. She stared at his hand as if it were an unpleasant foreign object. "A girlfriend would allow it," he added.

"I should have asked for more in the deal," she said.

"Too late. We Italians consider a pinky swear to be a legally binding contract," he said.

"That must explain why in every picture I've seen of Al Capone, he has locked pinkies with someone," Lou said. She caught sight of Vivian and Giovanni who were watching them with matching smiles of curiosity.

"When did this all come about?" Giovanni asked.

"Lou and I had a life and death moment in that elevator," Benny said. "It puts things in perspective."

"In an instant you can realize you're old and desperate and it's time to settle," Lou said. Vivian put her hand over her mouth and chortled.

"You're supposed to be on my side, Sister Vivian," Benny said.

"I'm confused. Aren't we all on the same side?" Giovanni asked.

"You would think so, wouldn't you?" Benny said. He checked his watch. "You know what time it is, Lou?"

She leaned over him and glanced at his watch. "Sylvester Stallone is pointing to the twelve and Arnold Schwarzenegger is pointing to the seven, so I guess that means it's go time."

"It's go time," he repeated and stood to gather everyone's attention.

CHAPTER 10

*L*ou was certain that, in all her thirty-two years, she had never been dirtier or more exhausted. She had sawdust and grime in places she didn't know existed previously. Though she tried hard to stay in shape and limber, nothing had prepared her for actual manual labor. Swimming laps and stretching were a far cry from building a structure. Her legs ached and her braces chafed, but she was so sore in her arms and abs the pain barely registered. In spite of all the pain, she was enjoying herself.

It was fun to be a part of a team, and even more fun to watch the Samperis in action. They were like a well-oiled machine and everyone fell into line behind them. Even Moss, about whom Lou had started to have serious doubts, was a consummate professional, fearlessly tackling jobs that seemed scary or dangerous to Lou. His ability to scale things was practically goat like, and his rapport with the people in the community who had come to help made her wonder if the Samperis were genetically programmed for world domination. Each of them seemed overloaded on charm, even Giovanni who was by far the most reserved member of the family.

By noon, the building was beginning to resemble what it was supposed to be. The frame was up, and it was time for a break. Lou went in search of Benny, who had been splitting his time between manning a saw and overseeing the teams. As she suspected, his face was drained of color and he was sweating profusely, even more than normal for such a hot day. She tapped him on the shoulder. He removed his ear protection.

"Come with me, Samperi," she said, crooking a finger at him. He followed her to a shady spot under one of the few surviving trees in town. The air was still and heavy, but at least they were out of the sun. Lou handed him a couple of bottles of water and a bagged lunch.

"You brought lunch for me?" he said, sounding pleased.

"Don't read too much into it; it's a humanitarian effort. Would you have stopped to eat on your own?" she asked.

"No, ma'am," he agreed. He patted the grass beside him. "Sit down, you're making me nervous."

"I can't sit on the ground," she said.

"Don't want to get your fancy pants dirty?" he guessed.

"Hello," she said, pointing out the grime all over her body. "I physically can't sit on the ground. My braces don't bend that way."

"Well, aren't I an idiot," he said.

"Yes," she agreed.

He laughed, stood, picked her up, and set her gently on the ground. "I'm never going to be able to get back up," she warned him.

"It's all right, we have access to a crane," he said.

"Oh, good. I was hoping we'd have a chance to bring in the heavy machinery. That should help me stay low key and fly under the radar." She lay down and closed her eyes. "How do you do this every day?"

"I don't work in the field much. I've been doing office stuff since I've been home. Everybody else hates paperwork, so it works out well," he said. He polished off his lunch and a bottle of water and lay down beside her. "I hate feeling weak. Before malaria I could work for days without rest. Now I'm tired from blinking."

"My body has been fighting me since the moment I was born, so take your sob story somewhere else," she said.

"I never thought of it that way. You make it seem so effortless," he said.

"If you pretend long enough, it becomes second nature," she said.

"That's good news for me," he said.

"How so?"

"Because right now you're pretending to be my girlfriend. Eventually you're going to forget you're pretending," he said.

"What's your end game here, Ben?" Lou asked.

He sighed and took her hand. "I don't know, Lou. But I know when I'm with you, everything feels okay again."

"So it's not so much a romantic attachment you have toward me as that of a toddler toward a binky," she said.

"I don't know," he repeated. "I don't know anything anymore."

"Here's my daily reminder you don't have to. No one expects you to have all the answers."

"There's where you're wrong. Everyone expects me to have all the answers," he said.

"I don't," Lou said. "In fact, I'm convinced you know absolutely nothing."

"I think that might be why I need you right now," Benny said. "I have nowhere to go but up in your estimation. With everyone else, it feels like I'm out on a precipice, waiting to fall and fail."

She patted his stomach. "Take comfort in the fact that I couldn't think lower of you."

He laughed. "That's another thing, Lou. Do you have any idea how long it's been since I laughed? I've seen so much bad." Abruptly, he stopped talking and shook his head.

She surprised them both by rolling toward him and hugging his waist. "Cheer up, chum. And when I say chum, I don't mean friend. I mean that bucket of fish guts they toss in the ocean to attract sharks."

"You're new to comforting people," he said, patting her.

"Maybe, but I'm expert level at distracting them from self-pity," she said. Her head was resting on his chest now, and his arm was around her. She could hear the steady thump of his heart, and it was soothing. After a few seconds of silence, she realized he was asleep. After about ten minutes of absolute stillness on her part, he woke with a start.

"I fell asleep," he said dumbly.

"Should you actually be here?" she asked.

"Probably not," he said. He yawned, rubbed his eyes, and checked his watch. "Yikes, I need to get back. Are you going to stay for a while?"

"Yes, please leave me helpless here like a beetle on its back," she said.

"Oh, right, I forgot. You make me forget things, Lou," he said. He reached for her, stumbled, and fell on top of her.

"That's going to leave a mark," she said, and he started to laugh, hard.

"Are you all right?" he gasped between laughter.

"I'd be better if I could breathe," she said, and he laughed even harder. "You're a sadist," she added and he gave up the pretense of trying to get back up. He collapsed on top of her and laughed until he couldn't catch a breath. "I could die under here, and no one would know until I started to smell, or maybe they'd think the smell was you. Geez, Samperi, there's nothing in the Bible against antiperspirant, even for missionaries."

"S-stop," he gasped. "I c-can't breathe."

"Aw, I feel so sorry for you. It must feel like having a giant man on top of you, crushing your sternum and deflating your lungs," she said.

"Lou, stop making me laugh," he pled. He swiped the tears off his face and rolled off her. "Are you all right?"

"Is it normal to see everything through a red haze?" she asked.

"For you, probably," he said. He stood up and reached down for her. "Let's try this again."

"Forget it, call in the crane," she said and he doubled over laughing again.

"I swear, Lou, you're better than therapy." He swiped his face again and reached for her. "For real this time."

"This must be how the women in a Jerry Lewis movie felt," she said. He sputtered a laugh but didn't give in to it. Instead he grasped her wrists and pulled her to a standing position in front of him. Before she could protest, he kissed her, gentle and sweet.

"Thanks for making me laugh," he said.

"Thanks for shattering my pelvis," she said, but she couldn't resist reaching on her toes for one more kiss. And that was how the resident, Analise, found them.

She cleared her throat delicately behind them. "Hi, Benny, you promised to go to the clinic with me today."

"Oh, I'm so sorry, Analise, I totally forgot," he said. "Is it all right if Lou comes with us?"

Lou did not want to go, and Analise did not want her to go. A little furrow developed between her perfect brows. "Oh, I don't..." she began. Benny gave Lou a squeeze, and she interrupted.

"I would love to see the clinic," she enthused, a lie. "To make sure my money's being put to good use."

"Your money?" Analise asked, one perfect eyebrow arching.

"This is Lou Lawton," Benny said. "Her company is funding the clinic."

"Oh," Analise said, disappointed. "Sure, the more, the merrier."

"Aren't you sweet?" Lou said, but the look that passed between the two women was anything but.

CHAPTER 11

*A*nalise's car was a tiny two seater. Lou stopped short when she saw it. "I can't sit in the back," she declared. It would be hard enough to cantilever herself into the low-slung front seat. Short of taking off her braces and crawling, there was no way she could stuff herself into the tiny back seat.

"I'll sit in the back," Benny reassured her with a squeeze of her hand. Analise gave her a haughty look that said she thought Lou was being a diva. Lou gave her a sweet smile in return, reassured by the fact that she would probably feel like a heel if she knew the truth. Or maybe she wouldn't. People had mixed reactions to the sight of Lou's braces. Some became effusive in their efforts to help while some became distant and cold, as if they thought Lou might be contagious. Either way, it was why Lou preferred to keep things hidden. As much as she could help it, she liked to keep her condition under wraps.

"Sorry, I know my car is kind of a dump. Med school loans. You must drive a Benz or something," Analise said, tossing Lou a catty smile.

"Or something," Lou agreed. In truth she drove a Honda that had been modified to compensate for the unpredictable weakness in her legs. And she hadn't learned to drive until after she graduated college and found someone who could modify a vehicle for her.

"My parents are immigrants," Analise continued. "I'm the first in my family to go to college, let alone med school."

"How wonderful," Lou said. "Good for you."

"No trust fund here," Analise added, with another catty smile.

Lou returned her smile. "I got a full scholarship to Princeton, so no trust fund needed."

"They must have given them out like candy, back in the day," Analise said.

"Undoubtedly," Lou agreed. "Although graduating summa cum laude was something I indisputably earned."

"And then you got a company for a graduation present," Analise said. "That's so nice."

"It was the best," Lou agreed. "And then I grew the company by forty percent, so my dad seemed pleased with the exchange."

"Um," Benny interrupted, but Lou touched her hand reassuringly to his cheek. The car was so tiny she didn't have to lean back to do so; he was right there.

"How long have you guys been together?" Analise asked.

"Good question," Lou said. She turned to Benny. "Hon?"

"We met when we were nine," Benny said slowly.

"He moved here from New York when his family had to flee the mob," Lou said. "Couldn't understand a word he said with that weird accent. We were all scared for our lives."

"We became best friends when we were twelve," Benny continued undaunted. "That continued for the next few years; we were practically always together."

"He stood me up for prom when we were seventeen," Lou interjected.

"She spent many years in bitter isolation while I traveled the world," he said.

"He got the monkey pox and had to come home," she added.

"And then she fell in love and began to pursue me," he said.

"And then he began treatment for mental delusions," Lou said.

"She cut the cables on her elevator and tried to kill me," Benny said.

"He made advances on me when I thought we were going to die," Lou said.

"She made advances back when it was clear we were going to live," Benny retorted.

"He blackmailed me and threatened to sue."

"She extorted me into an exclusive financial contract."

"He fell on me and crushed my spine," Lou said.

"And here we are," Benny finished. He took Lou's hand. "Very much in love."

"So much it hurts," Lou said, squeezing his hand until it became painful and he had to let go.

"Wow, that's something," Analise said. "Here we are." She parked in front of a cinderblock building that looked as if it had at one point functioned as a garage of some sort. People were already beginning to line up outside.

Lou couldn't get out of the car. Her braces, which were mostly to aid in walking, had little interest in helping her bend or crouch. Or get back up again if she did either of those things. There had been far too many times Lou had to take off her braces, stand up, and then put them back on again. She hoped she wouldn't have to do that now, but Benny came to her rescue. He climbed out Analise's side, came around, and lifted Lou from the car.

"How would you like a job as my personal shoehorn?" she asked him.

"What are the benefits?" he asked, his glance falling to her lips.

"We'll discuss the terms later," she told him, and he smiled. They followed Analise into the building. With no air circulation, it had become stifling. Benny rolled up the doors and people began to file in. Analise stood in the center of the room surrounded by some sparse medical equipment.

"No secretary?" Lou asked.

Analise frowned at her, hands on hips. "It's the middle of a disaster and they get residents on a week to week basis so, no, no one has thought to hire a secretary." She threw the word secretary out as if it were some kind of exotic luxury.

"Okay, little miss, enough attitude from you. Zip the lips and do what you do best and go doctor people. Leave the organization to me." Lou made a closing motion with her hands and turned to the waiting group. "Who here is healthy enough to lift a couple of things?"

A few of the men raised their hands.

"I want all of this equipment over there in the corner, except this table. I want this table in the entryway with a chair." The men began to do her bidding while Lou pulled out her phone and made a call. "Molly, I want you and Vivian to bring some supplies to the medical clinic. Get someone to drive you, if you don't know where it is. We need a few dozen bottles of water, some snacks, some magazines and toys, paper, and pens. And bring my laptop; it's in my suitcase. Thanks." She hung up the phone and stuffed it in her pocket. "Form a line. If you believe you have an emergency or a near emergency, I want you at the front." A couple of people shifted themselves to the front of the line. "Benny, take those forms and begin passing them out. If you could have everything filled out before you reach me, it would help a lot. We're going to get everyone through today, so don't worry. You will be seen, and hopefully as quickly as possible." She sat at the chair behind the table, picked up a pen, and spoke to the first person who had declared herself an emergency. "What seems to be the trouble today?"

Nearly six hours later, they were finished. Every patient had been seen, the clinic had been organized into a reception area, a waiting room with seating, snacks, and water, and an examination room, complete with canvas drop cloths serving as dividers. Molly started a spreadsheet on Lou's laptop and Vivian, who it turned out could type a hundred words per minute, entered every patient's contact information, along with Analise's diagnosis and follow up treatment recommendations. The women worked so well together that, after about an hour, Benny ended up leaving and going back to the construction site.

"Done," Lou announced after the last patient drove away. She, Molly, and Vivian high fived each other. She turned to Analise to include her in the camaraderie and was met with an icy stare. "Is something wrong, Analise?"

"Because you're paying for me to be here does not give you the right to embarrass me in front of my patients or come in here and take over," Analise said. Two bright spots of color stood in stark contrast to her dusky complexion.

"That was six hours ago," Lou said.

"It doesn't change the fact it happened," Analise said.

"You're right, and I apologize," Lou said. "I have a tendency to take over and organize when things are lacking organization. But I hope you can agree that, otherwise, we had a good day here."

"I do not agree," Analise said.

"All right," Lou said. "But you're still our ride back to the inn, unless you would prefer I ride strapped to the top of the car like a dead deer." Beside her, Vivian snickered and bit her lip to keep from laughing.

"It's fine, as long as you can stand to let your rich, precious self touch my crappy car," Analise said.

"Hey," Molly said, taking a step forward. "Lou's done nothing to deserve that kind of treatment from you."

"Yes, she has," Analise said.

"Don't worry about it," Lou told Molly. "I'd be thrilled to ride in your car, if you'll have me," she added to Analise. "Although I would still prefer to sit in the front seat."

"That's fine by me," Molly said.

"Me, too," Vivian declared.

"No," Analise said. "You already rode in the front seat. Let someone else have a turn."

"Hey," Molly said again, taking another step forward. Though gentle when it came to herself, she looked ready to brawl on Lou's behalf.

"It's really fine, Molly," Lou said. "Let's go, I'm starving." They stood by while Analise locked up the clinic. When they reached the car, Lou asked Vivian to hold her purse and laptop while she bent and unharnessed her leg braces so she could crawl into the back seat.

The ride back to the inn was tense and silent. "I'd like to speak to Lou a moment, please," Analise said when they arrived. Molly and Vivian filed out of the car. Molly hesitated, standing by to offer Lou a hand if needed.

"I'll be fine," Lou told her. "Go, eat." Reluctantly, the two women wandered to the hotel.

"Why didn't you tell me you had leg braces and that's why you couldn't sit in the back?" Analise asked.

"Would you like to walk around with your weaknesses on parade?" Lou said.

"You made me look bad in front of Vivian and Molly," Analise said.

"No, you did that to yourself," Lou said. "Let me tell you something, Analise. Being a woman in the professional world is hard. Carrying a chip on your shoulder makes it harder. I have no patience for girl drama, and you shouldn't either. It will weaken your cause and, eventually, it will weaken you."

"Thanks for the tip," Analise said, her tone bitter. "I guess you're going to tell Benny all about this."

"What I say to Benny is none of your concern, but please believe me when I tell you we have better things to talk about." She began the difficult journey out of the car, but before she could resort to crawling, Benny was there offering her a lift.

"Shoehorn," she greeted him with a smile. "Impeccable timing as always." Almost as soon as he levered her out of the car, Analise took off.

"Are you all right?" Benny asked. "I got an earful from Molly and Vivian. Apparently they believe Analise may be possessed by Satan."

"Meh, I've faced worse. Although I have to tell you I think you attract a certain brand of crazy," she said.

"Is that jealousy I hear?" he asked.

"No, that's valid concern for my safety, and yours. That girl is about one step from boiling someone's bunny," Lou said. "Hold still, I need to fasten these." She leaned on him while she stooped and reattached her leg braces.

He put his arm around her as they walked to the inn. "I saved you a plate because the food was going quickly and that's what good boyfriends do."

"Even fake ones?" she asked.

"Especially the fake ones," he said.

"You know what else fake boyfriends do?" Lou said.

"I'm ecstatic to find out," Benny said, his arm giving her waist a squeeze.

"They go swimming with their fake girlfriends," Lou said.

"Eh," Benny said. "Are you sure? I'm fairly certain that wasn't in the contract."

"Come on, it'll be fun," Lou said.

"Lou, I hate swimming."

"Still?"

"How would that have changed in the last decade? The places I've been, if you go swimming, you get eaten by a crocodile or an anaconda."

"And you don't like that?" she exclaimed. "Come on, Samperi. I haven't asked you for much, but I really, really need to go for a swim, and I would like it if you would come with me. This is me, opening my heart to you."

"Why does your heart have to be filled with chlorinated water?" he asked.

"The chlorination kills any softness or sentiment that might try to linger," she said. "I'm not going to beg here, but I am going swimming. So if you want to be with me, that's where I'll be."

"How deep is the pool?" he asked.

"It's only five and a half feet. You can touch the whole way."

"Touch what?" he said, turning to give her a smile that made her heart ping.

"Whatever you can catch," she said and, borrowing a move from his playbook, winked at him.

"Well, you did it, Lou. For the first time in my life, I'm really looking forward to going swimming. If you tell me you have a bikini, we can skip supper and go right now."

"I have a string bikini," she told him. "I didn't bring it, but I have one."

"It's cruel to give a man false hope," he said.

"I only wear my bikini at home. Too bad you're leaving the country soon, or I'd invite you for a swim," she said.

"For you in a bikini, I might postpone air travel indefinitely," he said.

"It's the 'might' that will ensure your invitation gets lost in the mail forever," she told him. "Let's eat, I'm starving."

"We have to wait a half hour before swimming."

"Not me, I like to live dangerously," she said.

"I bet you tear the tags off mattresses, too," he said.

"I'm adventurous, not psychotic, Mowgli," she said.

He squinted. "*The Jungle Book* references, is that where we're at now?"

"It was the best I could do on an empty stomach. Give me sustenance, and I'll come up with a zinger."

"From now on, I'm going to call whatever you eat 'sarcasm fuel,'" he said.

"I would also accept 'quick-wit juice' and 'insult power,'" she told him.

"You exhaust me," he said.

"I thought the malaria did that," she said.

"It's a tie," he said.

She stopped walking and kissed him, slowly and thoroughly.

"What was that for?" he asked when the kiss was finished. "Not that I'm complaining, mind."

"To give me an edge over the malaria," she said. "I've never liked a tie, it feels too much like losing."

"Lou, believe me—when it comes to obscure jungle fevers, the advantage is all yours," he said.

"I bet you say that to all your fake girlfriends."

"Just my Hattie Lou," he said, and kissed her again.

CHAPTER 12

"I thought you chickened out," Lou said. She had been swimming laps for a half hour when Benny finally arrived poolside. He sat on the edge and dangled his legs in the water.

"Those words aren't in my vocabulary," he said.

"That would explain your SAT score on the verbal," she said.

"That's not the way to entice me into the water," he said. On the edge of the pool, his knuckles looked a little white.

"How about this: if you drown, I promise to give you the best mouth to mouth of your life," she said.

"You know what people who don't like the water enjoy most? Drowning humor," he said.

She held out an arm. "Come on, Samperi. You can hold my hand the whole time."

He shook his head. "I want to hold something else."

Her hands shifted to her hips. "Get in the water, Benedict."

He slid off the wall and stood still for a moment, letting his body adjust to the coolness of the water. It was likely the pool was heated, but outside was so stifling anything felt cold in comparison.

She crooked her finger at him. "Come here."

"Come and get me," he said.

Lou rolled her eyes, but since she wasn't sure how deeply frightened he was, she walked forward and took his hand, tugging him further into the deep end. "Isn't this nice?" she prompted.

"Am I supposed to lie? You know I don't like the water."

"I can't fake date a man who doesn't like the water. It's a pretend deal breaker," she informed him.

"Why do I have to love it because you do?" he asked.

"Because I don't love it; I need it as part of my physical therapy. If I want to continue to walk, then I have to swim. A lot," she said.

"I didn't know that," he said.

"That's why I'm telling you," she said. They reached the deep end. He was nearly a foot taller than the top of the water, but still looked wary. Lou, who was only a couple of inches taller, had to tread water to stay afloat.

"How long can you do that?" he asked, eyeing her with calculated interest.

"I've never timed it, but probably a few hours," she said.

"Wouldn't it be easier to not tread water?" he asked.

"Are you trying to get me to drown myself? Because you're persuasive, but not that persuasive," she said.

He put his arms around her and pulled her close, holding her aloft. "Now this is nice."

"I'm only doing this to ease your anxieties," she told him as her arms slid around his neck.

"I also have a great fear of nudity. Is there anything you can do to help me with that?" he said.

"I only swim naked at home," she told him.

"I have *got* to see your pool," he said. She rested her palm on his cheek, searching his face for he knew not what. Lou was so rarely serious; Benny hated to break the spell. He remained perfectly still, enduring her perusal.

"What happened to you?" she whispered after a few minutes of intense silence.

"What do you mean?" he asked.

"Something broke you," she said. "What was it?"

He shook his head.

"Remember when we were best friends and you told me every-thing?" she prompted. "Pretend it's still like that."

He swallowed hard and looked away. "I don't think I can talk about it, Lou."

"Try."

"It wasn't one thing. It was an accumulation of things," he said. She petted his head, letting him speak in his own time. "Is the first time you watch a child die worse than the fiftieth time you see a child die? There was so much need, too much. So much horror. I started out believing I could change the world and ended up realizing I had let the world change me."

"I'm sorry," she said.

"No, see, that's the thing," he said, frustrated. "You can't be sorry for me when it's others who are the real victims. I am fine."

"But you're not," she said.

"But I should be," he argued.

"Why? Because you're better than everyone else? Because you're bigger, braver, more superhuman than the rest of us mere mortals? You're only one man, Benny."

"Then what's the point? What's the point of doing anything if nothing makes any difference?" he said.

"This is what you've never understood. Your entire life, you have never gotten what I'm about to tell you: There is making a difference, and then there's making *all* the difference. You cannot singlehandedly change the world, as much as I know you want to. You can plant the seed; you can do your part. But you have to realize, no matter what you do or where you are, you're a cog. And that's okay. Look at this week: You're rallying the troops, Molly is keeping everything on task, I'm paying the bills, your brothers are heading up construction, the teams are doing the grunt work of building, Analise is playing doctor, Sheila is our hostess extraordinaire, Charlie drove the bus."

"You know the bus driver's name?" he said, surprised.

"Who am I, Marie Antoinette? Of course I know the bus driver's name. Did you hear any of what I said to you? It takes a village to change the world. Recognize you are merely a villager, and take comfort in that fact. You're not singlehandedly going to save it, but you're not singlehandedly going to destroy it, either. We all have to do our part."

"Yes, my darling, I heard you. I always hear you. You have a way of speaking my language," he said, resting his forehead on hers. "Do I ever speak your language, Hattie Lou?"

"My language sounds a lot like a cash register dinging. Or perhaps the soft whir of a stock ticker," she said.

"*Cosa succede se lo dico in Italiano?*" he said. *What if I say it in Italian?*

"*Funziona davvero sulle donne?*" she returned. *Does that actually work on women?*

His jaw dropped. "When did you learn Italian?"

"College."

"Because of me?" he asked.

"Because of the Olive Garden. The unlimited breadsticks and I spent a lot of time together when I lived in New Jersey. But it's nice you have a rich fantasy life to keep you warm at night," she said. "Let's swim."

"I'd rather keep doing this," he said.

"Doing what? We're standing here. We could do this on dry land," she said.

"My point exactly," he said. "Let's."

"Come on," she coaxed. She took his hand and began urging him forward, but before he could move, Moss sprang from the darkness, landing on Benny so he went under, hard. Lou felt a panicky sort of helplessness as Benny went under and didn't resurface. Moss, on the other hand, swam off, completely unconcerned. Just when she planned to dive and retrieve him herself, someone from below dragged her underwater.

It was Benny, of course. There was no one else in the pool besides

Moss, who was now at the other end. He tugged her under and swam away, dolphinlike. After a few long strokes, he surfaced at the other end.

"You tricked me," she said.

"I learned a few things in college, too. Like how to swim," he said.

"You know, of course, this means war," she said, and they spent a long time chasing and dunking each other until they were interrupted by a loud gong. They turned to see Moss who had swum face first into the ladder at the approach of Molly.

"I take it Moss has never seen Molly in a swimsuit before," Lou said.

"More like Moss has never seen Molly as a girl before," Benny corrected.

"I can't believe you pretended you couldn't swim and were still afraid of the water," she said, remembering her earlier irritation with him. "You are such a rotten liar."

"I wasn't faking my dislike for the water. I learned to swim because of it. And I couldn't help myself. You were being so sweet, and warm, and caring. It was almost like you were a different person," he said.

"I don't have to take this abuse from you," she said.

"You're right. Go ahead and get out of the water," he said. She swam to the ladder and spent a long time struggling fruitlessly to climb out. "A little help?"

She nodded.

He went to the ladder and pulled her back to the water.

"What are you doing? I was getting out," she said.

"I've suddenly decided I enjoy swimming, as long as it's with you," he said, holding her close once more. "Also Analise is headed this way, and I need you to stay, pretty please."

There was another gong as Moss once more ran face first into the ladder at Analise's approach.

"Should he be allowed near the water?" Lou asked.

"Near the water, yes. Near women, no," Benny said.

"Look at you, being the perfect fake boyfriend by not even turning to see how good Analise looks in her swimsuit," Lou said. They were in a darkened corner of the pool, away from the light and the intrusive conversation of others. His arms were on her hips, and her hands were on his shoulders as they huddled together in their private little oasis.

"When I get done looking at you, I'm going to look at her. Maybe in another fifty years or so," Benny said.

"Were you born with these lines, or do you study them at night?" she said.

"Come on, I get no credit for that? It should be in a hall of fame somewhere," he said.

"I don't like lines; I prefer honesty," she told him.

"Then let me lay some honesty on you," he said. "Analise is a beautiful woman. The Latina thing works for her. But there is something completely and wildly captivating about you, and I can't look away. So I don't care if she's in a swimsuit or ball gown or naked or on fire because I would rather be here holding thirty two-year-old, CEO, wickedly sarcastic, pruny-fingered Hattie Lou Lawton."

"You didn't say I'm pretty," she said, affecting a pout, but she pulled him closer and plunged her fingers in his hair, her heart thudding painfully.

"Is there any way I can win with you, woman?" he asked.

"Probably not, but you should definitely keep trying," she said and pulled his palm close to kiss it.

"That's it? All I get is a lousy kiss on the palm?" he said.

"That's for later, to remember me by," she said.

"Are you packing off to 'Nam?" he asked. "Because I have a feeling we'll see each other again."

"Yes, but this is our secret," she said. "And this is our secret." She kissed his other palm. "And this is our secret." She pressed a kiss to the left of his Adam's apple, smiling when he swallowed hard.

"No more secrets?" he asked when she pulled away to look at him.

"One, but it's a big one. You have to let it build a bit," she said. They regarded each other in silence as the tension grew. Her thumb traced his lip, and at last she leaned in to whisper, her lips brushing his ear.

"*Ho imparato l'Italiano gratzie a te,*" *I learned Italian because of you.* With an impish smile, she dove under the water and swam away.

She needn't have swum so quickly. It took Benny a few seconds to recover. He remained staring mutely at the space she had been. Then, a slow smile spreading on his face, he dove under the water and swam after her.

CHAPTER 13

"**I**'ve been thinking," Moss said the next morning at breakfast.

"A dangerous pastime," Vivian said.

"I know," Giovanni added.

Molly laughed.

"What's so funny?" Moss asked.

"*Beauty and the Beast*," Molly said.

"Huh?" Moss said, his uncomprehending face a blank.

"Never mind," Giovanni said. "Continue. You've been thinking. I'm not sure you've ever said that before, so I'm genuinely curious about what's going to happen next."

The entire family, plus Lou and Molly, was gathered around the table that morning. Lou had unthinkingly retrieved Benny's coffee and fixed it the way he liked while he toasted her bread and applied the perfect amount of butter. Now they both sat quietly staring at their food, feeling slightly disquieted over the ease of their routine. Both were amazed by how quickly and easily they had resumed their once cozy relationship.

"I don't think Benny should go with us today," Moss said, and Benny's head snapped up.

"Not go? What are you talking about?" Benny said.

"I think you're overdoing it and you should take the day off or you might get sick," Moss said.

Giovanni held out his hand. "Phone."

"What?" Moss asked, trying and failing to look innocent.

"Let me see your phone," Giovanni said.

Moss leaned away from him. "No, that's private property."

"Yoink," Benny said, plucking the phone from Moss's other side. He scrolled through his texts until he found it. "Here it is, first page of his correspondence with Ma. 'I don't think Benny should be working so hard. He's going to get sick again. See what you can do to get him to stay behind.'"

"Wow, I didn't know you could imitate Ma so well. You sound exactly like her," Giovanni said, staring at his older brother in wonder.

Lou refrained from telling him what she knew—Benny was a whiz at impressions. As far as she knew, she was the only person who had heard that particular talent, and she felt a tad possessive of the information.

"Well, thanks, Ma and Puppet Moss, but I'm fine," Benny said.

"I'm with the ventriloquists on this one," Lou said.

"Lou, honey, baby, darling, beloved, did you forget I'm leading this particular venture?" he said.

"Benedict, my little snapping turtle, you don't have to have your finger in every pie. You have the lovely and talented Molly as your proxy. True leaders delegate," she said.

"I think it's important I be there," he said, his anger mounting. Everyone else at the table stared at him with something like awe. None of them besides Lou had ever heard him raise his voice before.

"I think it's important you remember you're a small cog in a large machine, totally and completely replaceable. Take a break. Let one of the other kids have a turn at bat," she said.

He frowned. "What do you want me to do? Sit in a lawn chair and eat grapes while everyone else works?"

"No. Molly, the itinerary, please." She held out her hand to Molly who, uncertainly, handed over the day's schedule. "You see here where you have yourself double booked for four hours? What's that about?"

"I was planning to go back and forth," he said.

"Pick one," she said.

"No," he said.

Smiling, she turned to the rest of the table. "Has Benny ever told you the limoncello story?"

"Lou," he exclaimed. "You can't tell them that."

"We were fifteen, and…" she began, but he put his hand over her mouth.

"This one, I pick this one. But you're coming with me," he said.

"Fine," she said. If she were being honest, she could use a break from construction, too. Her legs were so sore every step was painful, even after the long swim the night before.

"Wait, what's the limoncello story?" Moss asked. "I might literally die if I don't find out."

"You've had a good run," Giovanni said. "But what is the limoncello story?"

"Lou, you got what you wanted. Do not tell that story," Benny said, his eyes pleading.

She was tempted to tell it anyway. It was nothing more than run-of-the-mill teenage hijinks, but for Benny, who had tried so hard to be perfect, it loomed large as a glaring character fault. Which was more important to her? To tell a funny story or to protect Benny's self-imposed sterling reputation? She held out her pinky to Benny who squeezed it with his, sighing with relief.

"Sorry, guys," she told a disappointed Giovanni and Moss. "It stays in the vault. A pinky swear is legally binding for Italians."

"I didn't know that," Moss said.

"It went all the way to the Supreme Court," Giovanni said. "The Ferraris sued the Fiats over a meatball recipe. I can't believe you never heard about it."

"Now that you mention it, it does sound kind of familiar," Moss said.

"Ask around," Giovanni encouraged. "I bet everybody has heard of it but you."

Everyone else studiously stared at their plates, not daring to make eye contact with anyone else.

"You all make me glad I only have a sister sometimes," Vivian said after Moss got up to retrieve more cereal.

"You should try being an only child," Lou chimed in. "It's spectacular." She rested her hand on Benny's leg and gave it a squeeze, her signal asking if they were okay. He laid his hand on hers and squeezed back, his signal they were.

Moss returned with his cereal. "Hey, I asked like five people about the meatball Supreme Court thing, and no one has heard of it."

"It's probably because they're not Italian. Next time we go back to Brooklyn, bring it up in the neighborhood. I bet it will get a big reaction," Giovanni said.

"I'll probably forget by then," Moss said.

"I promise to remind you," Giovanni said.

"All right, thanks," Moss said.

"What are brothers for?" Giovanni said.

"Not this," Vivian said. "Moss…"

Giovanni leaned forward and pressed his lips to hers.

"You can't kiss me forever," she said when he pulled away.

"I can kiss you until you forget," he said, and kissed her again.

"Forget what?" she said when the second kiss was finished.

"So you guys, like, make out at breakfast now?" Moss said, spooning cereal into his mouth as he watched them kiss.

"It's not actually a new thing, but you're not usually with us when we're at breakfast," Giovanni said.

"I've tried, but you keep sending me away," Moss said. He turned to Benny and Lou. "Are you guys going to get in on this, or is there an age limit? Like after thirty you're not allowed to kiss until sundown or something."

"As I was saying, being an only child is the way to go," Lou said.

"Molly's an only child," Moss said, and everyone turned to look at him. "What?"

"I think everyone's a bit in shock you know personal, detailed information about me," Molly said.

"You've been our secretary for three years. I'm not a moron," Moss said, and Giovanni choked on a sip of coffee.

"It's okay to let some of them go," Vivian told him, rubbing his back gently until he got his windpipe back under control.

"Molly, I guess you're in charge today," Benny said, his tone somewhere between resigned and resentful.

"How come I'm never in charge?" Moss asked.

"You can be in charge of making sure people have fun," Benny said, ever the diplomat. "And Giovanni can be in charge of making sure everyone has the proper tools for the job. Molly is in charge of keeping everyone on task and getting everyone there and back. And Vivian is in charge of making sure Moss and Giovanni don't quarrel the whole time."

"I feel my job is the hardest," Vivian said. "But I'll soldier on."

Benny and Lou waved to them as they left to head for the bus. "What's my job today?" Lou asked when they were alone at the table.

"To do whatever I tell you without question," he said, and she laughed.

"I forgot how funny you are," she said.

"I'm serious, Lou. You're making me take it easy today; this is your penance."

"I thought my penance was coming on this trip in the first place. And then having to pretend to be your girlfriend," she said.

He draped his arm around her shoulders. "Has that been such a hard job?"

"Insufferable," she said, leaning forward to kiss the tip of his nose.

"Today is going to be physically easier, but still a different kind of exhausting," he said. "It would help if I knew you were fully on board as my co-pilot."

"Why don't you tell me what we're going to be doing, and then I will tell you if I'm willing to be Sonny to your Cher," she said.

"The pastor of the church who has been coordinating the relief efforts gave me a list of community members who, though their houses weren't destroyed, were still somehow affected by the storm.

It's our job to visit them and see if they qualify for a relief check from your company."

She wrinkled her nose. "I don't like having to deal with needy people directly; that's why I set up a foundation. It's too hard to personally decide who gets money and who doesn't."

"That's why I need you on board. I'll have the final say about who gets a check," he said.

"Your heart is the size of the moon. Everyone gets a check in your world."

"Is that such a bad thing?" he asked.

"No."

"I'm glad to hear you say that, but you're wrong. I've become adept at discerning who is needy and who is gaming the system. So if I say someone doesn't get a check and you say they do, then we'll go with my decision," he said.

"And what if I say someone doesn't get a check and you say they do?" she asked.

"Then we go with my decision," he said.

"Is this some sort of power play because I made you stand down from construction today?" she asked.

"Believe it or not, my baby, this is me protecting you."

"From what?" she asked.

"You'll see," he said. He took her hand, helped her stand, and they were on their way.

CHAPTER 14

The pastor lent them his car, gave them a county map, and told them to be careful. Lou thought it was merely a polite thing people said, until they started driving. The hills and hollers of Appalachia were not for the faint of heart, as Lou soon realized. She was thankful Benny was adept at navigating the terrain. The county map soon made sense when it became clear many of the roads and houses they were visiting either weren't on GPS or weren't named.

"You know what this reminds me of?" Lou said.

"The fifth circle of hell?" Benny guessed.

"No, *this* reminds me of high school. Remember that summer you got your license and wanted to drive all the time, but your mom would only let you drive on a few back roads? So on your days off you'd pick me up in your dad's truck, and we'd drive for hours around those same few country roads."

"That was fun," he said.

"That was fun," she agreed.

"I can't believe we never fooled around," he said. "Two kids, completely unsupervised for hours at a time, driving by endless abandoned barns. What a wasted opportunity."

"We did, remember? We went in that abandoned barn and were there for hours and hours. Oh, wait, that was someone else. Never mind," she said, poking his leg.

"Let me guess: my cousin Mateo?" he said.

"You really have to let that go," she said. "It was one little kiss."

"Your first kiss?" he guessed.

She shrugged.

He faced forward, scowling. "I'm going to punch him in the face this Thanksgiving."

"I assumed that's what you Samperis always do on Thanksgiving," she said.

"I've been thinking about what you said," he said.

"What did I say?"

"The piece of advice you gave me, the good one," he said.

"You're going to have to narrow it down," she said. "All my advice is good."

"Last night, when you told me I'm only a tiny cog in a large machine. I've been replaying that, and it's brought me a lot of comfort. The last few months have been…difficult. I've been feeling a lot of burnout. Realizing I'm only a little piece of a big puzzle has been strangely healing. It makes me feel like I'm ready to get back on the horse."

"I'm glad to hear you're finding some peace emotionally, but Benny, you seem to have a long way to go in your physical recovery," she said.

"I'm fine," he said, frowning.

"I get it, it's no fun to be sick or weaker than you want to be. But pushing yourself too far too fast will have terrible consequences. Take it from someone who is the queen of pushing herself too hard. Every time I do it, I end up back in my wheelchair for a few days. No fun."

"I'm fine," he insisted.

"Prove it," she said.

He turned to her with a smile. "What did you have in mind, Lou?"

"Pull over and bench press this car."

"I can't bench press this car," he said.

"See? You are not fine."

"No one can bench press a car," he argued.

"Where's that can-do attitude I used to know and love? Age has changed you," she said.

"Lucky for us, age hasn't changed you one bit," he said.

"It's changed me plenty," she said.

"How? You're exactly as feisty and funny as I remember," he said.

"I used to be a lot more openhearted and trusting," she said.

He winced. "Lou, please let's talk about prom."

"Benny, please stop thinking you're the only person in my life I'm referring to," she said. "Lots of people have chewed me up and spit me out. It's only by some miracle I have remained as sweet and gentle as I am."

"You're as sweet and gentle as a porcupine walking backwards," he said. "We appear to be here." He parked the car and turned it off. Lou turned to survey the scene.

"I'm going to give them money," she said.

"You can't give them money based on appearances," he said.

"But it's a wooden shack covered in tar paper," she said.

"Some people like it that way," he said.

"Who could like it that way?" she asked.

"Lou, please don't take what I'm about to tell you the wrong way because I know you have a big heart, beneath all the pretense. But you have a limited life perspective. You're rich; you grew up rich, you've been surrounded by other rich people your entire life. There's a whole other way of life out there you've never experienced, people scrambling to make a living and taking pride in the little bit they have. If you go in and offer them money off the bat, you might offend them."

"People would be offended by having money offered to them?" she asked.

"Some. You have to meet them at their level, get to know them a little, find out what the real need is. It's not always money. In fact, it almost never is. Most people are simply dying for someone to care."

"All right," she said.

"That seemed too easy. You never let me win that easy," he said.

"I've been a boss for a long time, and one thing I've realized is the best bosses admit when they don't know enough to make an informed decision. This is your area of expertise; I'm willing to defer to you," she said.

He blinked at her, surprised. "You never cease to amaze, Lou. What else can I get you to defer about, as long as you're in this mood?"

"Don't press your luck, Samperi," she said. He came around and helped her out of the low-slung car and they approached the house together.

A stooped, white haired woman opened the door at Benny's knock. "Y'all sellin' somethin'?" She had a deep, hills accent, discernable only because they had been in Kentucky long enough to parse through it.

"No, Ma'am," Benny replied. His accent was an 80/20 mix of Brooklyn and Kentucky, but he could swing it either way he wanted. Now he sounded almost native and Lou had to remind herself his chameleon nature was an essential tool of blending in and not a way of being fake. "We're checking on people after the storm, seeing if you have any needs we might relay to the local pastor."

"Oh," the woman said, surprised. "Well, come in then, I guess."

They followed her into the ramshackle little structure and sat on a settee while she claimed the lone recliner.

"Y'all want tea?" she asked.

Lou was about to refuse, but Benny preempted her. "We'd love some, but I can get it, if you tell me where the glasses are."

"The cupboard to the left of the sink," she said, seeming relieved she didn't have to get up again. "Thank ya', hon.'" Benny left the room and the woman bestowed her attention on Lou. "You're a right purdy little thing."

"Thank you," Lou said, smiling. "Have you lived here long?"

"All my life, and my parents before me."

"Never married?" Lou chanced.

"Married three times and buried all of them. I have nine children."

"Oh, my lands," Lou said. "How did you manage that?"

"Like everything, the best I could," she said.

"Did you see the tornado?" Lou asked.

"No, ma'am. Didn't even know about it 'til one of my kids came to check on me," she said. "Lost all my chickens. The wind came down and—whoosh—they were gone."

"I'm sorry to hear that," Lou said.

The woman shrugged. "They was pretty stupid, but I miss those eggs. Nothing like fresh eggs to keep a body strong, unless it's fresh milk, but that's harder to come by these days."

"I've never had fresh milk," Lou said.

"Nothin' like it," the woman declared. "We used to have a cow, and I would nip out to the barn every morning for a bit. Sometimes I took more than my share, and my daddy blamed the cow for running dry. But it was too much temptation for a hungry little girl to withstand."

"Yes'M," Lou commented as Benny returned with their drinks. "She lost her chickens in the storm, Ben."

"What a shame," Benny agreed. "Coop and all?"

"Coop and all, though after what others lost, it seems wrong to bellyache about a few lost feathers and eggs," she said.

Lou gave Benny a questioning look. He gave a slight nod in reply. "Ma'am, we'd like to help you replace those chickens, and your coop," Ben said.

"How y'all plan to do that?" the woman asked.

"With a check," Ben said.

She gave them a skeptical look. "This some kind of scam?"

"No, ma'am. We'll write you a check, free and clear. It's part of our work this week in the community, helping to rebuild and such."

"Where's the money come from?" she asked.

Benny looked to Lou. "A charitable foundation that specializes in community rebuilding," she said.

"Well, I suppose," the woman said, still scratching her head in dismay.

Lou whipped out her company's checkbook and wrote the check before Benny could offer his input. She tore the check from the book and handed it over. The woman's eyes bugged when she read the amount.

"We'll see ourselves out. Have a nice day, and thank you for the tea," Lou said. She took a few sips of the cool, refreshing tea and set it back on its coaster. The woman made no reply as Lou and Benny made their exit.

"Lou, you gave her five thousand dollars," Benny hissed once they were outside.

"How do I know how much chickens or coops are?" she said.

"You know they're less than that," he said.

"Now she can get a really nice one, maybe a chicken condo or such, something with a pool."

"Lou," he said, exasperated.

"What? We're here to give people money, aren't we?"

"At this rate you won't have any left when we're finished," he said.

She laughed. "You clearly have no idea of my net worth."

That gave him pause. "What is your net worth?"

"Enough for all the chicken coops in the world," she told him.

He frowned. "I've never been with a woman who made more than I did."

"I've never been with a man who made less," she said, smiling when his frown deepened.

"I don't like that," Benny said.

"Which part, that I'm wealthier than you imagined or that I've dated other men?"

"Which one do you think?" he asked.

"I think it goes against your superman persona to realize you're not the wealthiest, most altruistic person in the world. And you're jealous of the unknown men I might have dated."

"Aren't you jealous of the unknown women I might have dated?" he asked.

"No."

"Why not?" he asked.

"If they meant anything to you, you wouldn't be here with me," she said.

"That's really aggravating, you know," Benny said.

"I'm sorry my maturity and security annoy you," she said.

"I accept your apology," he said, kissing her forehead as he tucked her into the car.

CHAPTER 15

They visited several more houses, and each one was a learning experience for Lou. Benny was right; she would have given money to everyone. They ended up giving money to only one more, at Benny's insistence. One had no storm damage and another said they had storm damage but couldn't agree on what it was. When Lou questioned Benny later, he told her they were quite possibly cooking meth in the back room. They hadn't stayed there long.

As they pulled up to the last house on their list, Lou wondered if she had the energy to go inside. Today's exhaustion was a whole different sort than the type she'd faced after a long day of construction. Meeting people, being exposed to a lifestyle so different than her own, and trying to discern true need was enough to make her brain hurt.

"Last one, Lawton," Benny said, though he sounded as tired as she felt.

"We're pathetic," Lou said. "We're thirty two and have the combined energy of a ninety year old."

"One more house and we can go home and complain about kids on our lawn," he said.

"One more house," she said. She tried to lever herself out of the car, but couldn't. Benny came around to pull her out, and it took him a few tries, as well. Once she was finally out, they stood by the car for a minute, heads together, trying to regain some energy.

"I wonder how much it would cost to buy a helper monkey," Lou mused.

"Monkeys aren't all they're cracked up to be. The ones in Suriname routinely stuck their hands in my windows and stole things," he said. "Plus they're loud and smelly."

"Mine would be polite and toilet trained," she said. "But I suppose if you're really against it, I'll set aside my well thought out monkey plan for a while."

"I think it's for the best," he agreed. "Ready?"

"Ready," she said. They took a step toward the house and froze as a scream rent the air.

"Hello?" Benny called, and the scream came again, along with the sound of a woman sobbing. He ascended the porch steps quickly and knocked on the door. Lou hobbled behind him. He tried the handle. "Locked. Hello? Is everyone okay in there?"

They could hear furiously murmured words, as if two people were arguing, and then the crying came again. Finally, a plaintive, "Help me."

"You have to break down the door," Lou said.

"I get winded reaching for my wallet, and you think I have the strength to break down a door? Has my malaria taught you nothing?" he said.

"I'll break down the door," she said

"With what? You can't break a door down with stubbornness and pride," he said.

She scanned the horizon, saw a window to their right, and it was open. "There. You have to shimmy through that window."

"I know I've lost weight since I've been sick, but I still have bones. There is no way I can fit through that window," he said.

"Then I'll do it. Shove me through."

"Lou, you need to take a breath and settle. All your plans are bad when you get worked up," he said.

"Benny, someone could be dying while you're standing there telling me to calm myself which, in case you are unfamiliar with all of womankind, has never worked since Adam told Eve to take a deep breath and put down the apple."

"You're essentially telling me to help you break into someone's house," he said.

"To help them," Lou said.

"What if they don't see it that way? Do you know how many guns the average homeowner has in this part of the state?"

"No, do you?"

"No, but I don't want to find out," he said.

They heard more crying from inside. "Give me a boost," she demanded.

"Fine, but I'm going on the record by saying this is a terrible idea."

"Duly noted," she said. He tried to dead lift her through the window but couldn't. She was slim, but she was also tall. Next he knelt and tried to grab her foot and give her a boost, but her braces wouldn't allow her foot to bend that way. Finally he knelt and let her use his back as a table, counting on her swimming-induced upper arm strength to pull her through.

When she was about halfway through the window, with the sill cutting painfully into her midsection, she looked up to see an old man in a wheelchair staring at her.

"Well, hey there," Lou said.

He nodded.

"I heard some screaming," she continued.

He pointed to the television, currently playing a Mexican soap opera. "My stories," he explained.

"Uh-oh," Lou said. Benny stood and gave her a final shove through the window. Her arms windmilled wildly in the air for a few seconds, and then she plunged face first toward the floor, landing hard on her wrists and elbows.

"Lou, what's going on?" Benny hissed from beneath the window.

"Everything's fine," she assured him with no idea how she was going to get off the floor. She tipped her head up and looked at the man who was now upside down to her. "How would you like some money?"

"I wouldn't complain," he said.

"Great," Lou replied. She sat up, unbuckled her braces, used a nearby chair to pull herself up, and reattached her braces. She pulled out her checkbook, had a conversation, wrote the man a check, and let herself out the front door.

Benny stood leaning on the car, smiling a little self-satisfied smile. "How did it go?"

"The situation is all sorted out, he was incredibly grateful for my help. Let's go," she said.

He made no move to get out of her way, and he was leaning on her door. "What was the problem in there? Was someone dying?"

"Yes."

"And you stopped it," he said.

"I can be incredibly persuasive," she said.

"Now you're preaching to the choir," he said. "Should I call the newspaper, alert the evening news about your heroism?"

"I want no credit; it's enough I've done my good deed," she said. "Let's go."

"You can't do it, can you?" he asked.

"Do what?"

"Admit you were wrong, say I was right," he said.

"Of course I can, and if it ever happens, you'll be the first to find out," she said, reaching out a hand to pat his chest. He grabbed the hand and used it to draw her closer until they were toe to toe.

"We're not leaving until you admit I was right," he said.

"I've made my peace with living here forever," Lou said.

He slipped his arms around her and began gently rubbing her back. Lou began to melt a little and leaned into him for support. "Which is more difficult, admitting you were wrong or admitting I was right?"

"I don't know what you're talking about, they're both my favorite," she said.

"Lou, confession is good for the soul," he said.

"I hear a vegan diet is, too, but I have no desire to try that, either."

"Say it, say the words." He moved her bottom lip as he said, "Benny was right, and I was wrong."

"If you don't believe me, go ask him," Lou said, shooing his hand away from her face.

"You want me to go ask the person in that house if you saved his life?"

"More than anything," she said.

"Fine, I will," he said. He sidestepped her, jogged up the porch steps, knocked on the door, and let himself in when the man called for him to enter. A few minutes later, he returned looking mutinous. "Get in the car, Lou."

For once, she did as she was told, staying mum as he slid behind the wheel and buckled up. He drove for about fifteen minutes before he finally spoke. "I cannot believe you paid him off to lie for you."

"I didn't," she said.

"You did, you foxy little liar," he said.

"Did you call me foxy? Are we in a black and white movie from the forties now, dollface?"

"Don't you dare try to change the subject. You paid that old man to tell me you saved his life. At the very least have the decency to admit that," he said.

She took a deep breath and clasped her hands in her lap. "Benedict, I paid the man because he has an infected wisdom tooth that, if he doesn't have removed, will most likely turn septic and kill him, at least according to his doctor, with whom he had an appointment yesterday. Without my money, he had no way to pay for the surgery. Hence, I saved his life today," she said.

He skidded to the side of the road and threw the car into park. "That is…you are…sometimes I don't know if I want to kiss you or punch you." He grabbed her, pulled her to him, and kissed her, deeply and thoroughly.

At last they pulled apart, breathing hard and about to suffocate in the hot car. "You kiss okay, but I've had better punches," she said.

He banged his head on the steering wheel a few times until the horn honked. "What does it take to leave you speechless?" he yelled.

"You don't want to know," she said.

"Yes, I very much do," he replied.

"Laryngitis," she replied. She opened her mouth to say something else, but he made a closing motion with his hand.

"Not another word. You know what I'm going to do?"

"Do you?" she asked.

"I'll show you what I'm going to do, something I should have done years ago." He threw the car into gear and began to drive, speeding toward she knew not where. At last he parked in front of a ramshackle old barn and turned off the car.

"Is this the part where you confess your good guy act has been a façade and you've brought me here to kill me and hide the body?" Lou asked.

"No, this is the part where we go back in time, right a wrong, and do what we should have done when we were sixteen," he said.

"Realize we had the raging metabolism of toddlers and could have eaten whatever we wanted?" she guessed.

"We're going in the barn," he said. "And we're not coming out for a good, long while."

"What are we going to do while we're in there?" she asked, heart thumping.

"Discuss philosophy," he said. "What else?" He hopped out of the car and came around to get her. He opened her door and held out his hand to help her out.

She stared at the hand. "If we were really sixteen, I would wheel myself in with my chair," she said, allowing him to take her hand and pull her from the car.

He shook his head. "I would have carried you."

"Why don't you carry me now?" she said.

"Malaria. I guess you could lie down and I could drag you in by one arm," he said.

"That sounds like a different sort of fantasy," she said. "How about if I walk in and lean on a beam for support?"

"Perfect," he said. They walked to the barn hand in hand.

"Do you think we would have held hands when we were sixteen?" she asked. "We didn't do a lot of touching back then."

"We're righting old wrongs. If I could go back and do our teenage years over, I would never not be touching you," he said.

"That would have made for some awkward trips to the men's room," she said. He pushed open the door and they stepped inside. Little rodent feet scurried for cover, and Lou tried not to sneeze at all the mold, hay dust, and cobwebs in the air. "This place looks like it's thirty seconds from toppling over. Is this safe?"

"That's not what you would have said when we were sixteen," Benny chided.

"Back then I probably would have said we should carve a scary message in a beam for anyone who comes after us. That still sounds like a good idea, by the way. Something like 'I saw what you did.'"

They walked to the center of the barn. She leaned against a beam, and he stood in front of her. "So, Lou, now that we're sixteen, I've been doing a lot of thinking."

"Me, too. Have you heard of these new things called cellular phones? I think they're a dying fad," she said.

"You're ruining it. Play along," he coaxed.

"Fine. I'm super nervous about my pre-calc exam tomorrow."

"Me, too," he agreed.

"You don't take that class," she said.

"I'm nervous for you. But I've been thinking about other stuff."

"What kind of other stuff?" she asked.

"Well, like how my little brothers are driving me crazy," he began, but she interrupted.

"Are you still being sixteen? Because that could be true today."

"It works on a lot of levels. But lately I've been thinking maybe you and I should, you know, kiss."

"We've been friends for ages. Why all of a sudden have you been thinking that?" she asked.

"Because lately I see you in the hall and everything goes stupid, and all I can think is how much I want to touch you," he said.

"That's an interesting proposition, Samperi, but we're best friends. What if it messes everything up?" she said.

"Let's try," he urged. "I'll teach you how."

"Your cousin," she began, but he put his finger to her lips.

"Sixteen-year-old me would not have been able to handle the information about Mateo."

"Baby, thirty-two-year-old you doesn't seem to be able to handle it, either," she informed him. "How many people had sixteen-year-old you kissed?"

He squinted, trying to remember. "Two, but I didn't much enjoy it."

"What makes you think it would have been better with me?" she asked.

"Because everything is better with you," he said. "Now, back to being sixteen. Put your hands here." He placed her hands on his chest. "And I'll put my hands here." He placed his hands on her hips, his thumbs smoothing over her hipbones.

"Now what?" she whispered. She wasn't sure if she was whispering because she didn't want to disturb whatever animals might inhabit the barn or because she was actually getting into their pretend scenario. Either way, her heart was thumping hard against her chest, exactly as it would have done if sixteen-year-old Benny were about to kiss her.

"Just this," he said and kissed her, a sweet and gentle kiss, the exact kiss he would have given her as her sixteen-year-old best friend. But they weren't sixteen anymore, and they were alone, utterly and completely alone for the first time in days. It was Lou who intensified the kiss, slipping her hands behind his head and pulling him closer while arching her body upward, trying to meld herself into him. Benny's lips trailed to her neck, his hand lifted her hip.

"This might have been a bad idea," he whispered.

"No, this is the best idea you've ever had," she said, and then the shot rang out.

CHAPTER 16

They whirled to see a man standing approximately fifteen feet away, holding a shotgun.

"Y'all are trespassing," he announced.

Lou opened her mouth to apologize, but Benny let her go and began to advance on the man. "Are you insane? You could have killed her."

"I had every right; you're intrudin' on private property," the man said.

"You're not allowed to kill someone for standing in an empty barn," Benny yelled. Lou had never seen him so angry.

She tugged his arm. "Benny, it's fine, let's leave."

"No," he yanked his arm free and resumed upbraiding the man, taking a step closer. "You might feel powerful because you have a gun, but if you'd like a real challenge, why don't you drop it and see what happens?"

"Why would I do that?" the man asked, perplexed.

Benny took another step forward, and Lou physically inserted herself in front of him. "Okay, easy there. We're super sorry we were kissing in your barn, mister. Bye." She grabbed Benny's arm and pulled him out of the building and to the car.

"Can you drive?" she asked.

He nodded, still scowling, started the car and took off down the long, dirt road.

"What was that?" she asked after a few minutes of tense silence.

"What do you think? That man threatened your safety. He could have killed you," he said.

"He could have killed *you*," she pointed out.

He cast her a disparaging glance. "You've met my family. You think a gun scares me?"

"I think it should," she said. "Especially when wielded by the less intelligent character from *Of Mice And Men*." She ran her hand soothingly down his arm. "It's sweet and kind of weird you went postal and tried to protect me, but you can't go around doing stuff like that. You can't fly off the handle."

Now he gave her his full attention. "You're lecturing me about not flying off the handle?"

"What are you talking about? Do you realize how calm I have to be in my job? People respond to my tone, and so my tone has to be measured and serene. I've worked hard to make it so across the board, in every avenue of my life," she said.

"Have you met you?" he said.

She laughed. "You're nuts. I mean, I'll admit maybe in our youth I was a bit feisty, but I've mellowed."

"Lou, a poked hornet's nest is a little feisty. You're a whole other level," he said.

"You're funny," Lou said, her tone and smile equally indulgent.

"And you're something else," Benny said. They arrived back at the hotel and walked up the porch steps. Benny stopped short and put his hand to his head. "I forgot my notes on the day to give to the pastor. Will you wait here for me?"

"Sure," Lou said, leaning against one of the porch's stately columns. She felt the sort of bone weariness that could come from a long day of emotional and physical exhaustion. It was a bad time for Analise to approach but, in retrospect, Lou thought there probably was no good time.

"Did you tell him?" Analise asked.

"Tell who what?" Lou asked, barely suppressing a yawn. Her legs ached, her arms ached from falling through the window, and she was hungry and thirsty.

"Don't play stupid," Analise said.

"Apparently it's not an act because I have no idea what you're talking about," Lou said. She wished her phone's battery hadn't recently run out; it was an ideal time to catch up on messages and tune the doctor out.

"I know you told Benny what happened between us in the car. He's been avoiding me," Analise said.

"He's been busy," Lou said.

"No, it's because you pushed him away from me," Analise said.

"A stiff wind could push him away from you," Lou said. "He's not interested. Take the hint, sister wife."

"You're only saying that because you're intimidated."

Lou stood upright away from the column. "Intimidated? And why, exactly, would I be intimidated by you?"

"Because I'm younger, prettier, smarter, and a better match for him."

"Are you on any sort of medication we should be aware of?" Lou asked.

"No, I'm serious. I'm going to be a missionary doctor. Benny and I are a perfect match, he's the entire reason I requested to come on this trip. Nobody mentioned anything about a girlfriend, and then you miraculously show up and ruin everything. And I don't even think you really like him that much, so why don't you go away and let someone else have a chance."

"You know, I've tried to take the high road, considering my four years of advanced age, but you're a hot mess, and I'm done. So if you would like to settle this like we're still in the schoolyard, say the word."

She said a word, a nasty word Lou had never called another woman. "That's it," Lou said. She was bent over unfastening her brace when Benny arrived on the scene.

"What's going on?" he asked, his tone wary.

"I'm taking off my leg brace so I can beat her with it," Lou said.

"Why?" Benny asked.

"Because she's probably faster, and I need a weapon of some sort." She removed the brace, held it aloft, and took a step toward Analise who backed away uncertainly.

Benny caught her around the waist and held her back. "You can't beat her up, Lou."

"I'm fairly certain I can, I have a few inches on her," Lou said.

"I mean you *shouldn't* beat her up," Benny said.

"She's crazy," Analise interjected. "We were standing here talking, and she went all insane on me."

"You should go," Benny said.

"But…" she began.

"Do you want me to let Lou go?" he asked. "Because once she gets started, she won't quit. She's like a badger that way."

Frowning, Analise turned and slunk inside. Lou waited until she was gone to safely reattach her brace.

"Tell me again how it's best not to fly off the handle," Benny said.

"This is different. She had it coming," Lou said.

"I agree, that girl is all kinds of deranged," Benny said.

It should have heartened Lou that he automatically took her side, but it didn't. "I have a question for you," she said, straightening.

"Fire away."

"You wanted me to cover you so Analise wouldn't chase you, but I think my presence here has actually spurred her on. So who exactly are we still pretending for?" she asked.

"Are we still pretending, Lou? Or are we only pretending to pretend?"

"I don't know anymore," she said.

"Maybe we should live in the moment, see where things go," he suggested.

"And when you go back to saving the world, what then?" she asked.

"We'll cross that bridge when we get there," he said.

"I can't do that, Ben," she said.

"Why not?"

"Because I'm not a placeholder until a better offer comes along," she said. "Even when the other offer is a noble good deed."

"There's something between us," Benny said.

"An old friendship and a little bit of attraction," Lou said.

"A current friendship and a galaxy of attraction," he amended.

"Speak for yourself," she said.

"I am," he replied. "I want to be with you, Lou."

"Enough to say you'll stay in the states for the long haul?" she asked. When he didn't answer, she turned and went inside.

CHAPTER 17

*A*fter a quiet supper, Lou turned in early. Her leg muscles were exhausted to the point of uncontrollable wobbling. They would be better after rest, she knew, but the real reason she went to bed was because she lacked the energy to face Benny again. They'd had such a pleasant day until the end. Why had she felt the need to ruin it by getting real? Why couldn't she have continued to play along and pretend?

She slept through the night and woke late with barely enough time to shower and dry her hair before tossing down a quick breakfast. There were a few other stragglers at her table, the teenage jock and bookworm among them.

"How did you come to be on the trip?" Lou asked them.

"Miss Haslett, I mean Mrs. Samperi, was my school librarian," the girl said. "I was one of her student assistants. It was kind of awesome because it got me out of gym."

"Why would you not want to do gym?" the boy asked. His name was Eli and the girl's name was Shayna.

"It's only like the worst thing ever," Shayna said.

"Gym is the best. It's a cake class," Eli said.

"If you like running around, climbing a rope, and doing endless pushups," Shayna said.

"What's wrong with any of that?" Eli asked.

Shayna rolled her eyes. "Eli, you are such a jock."

"How are you guys enjoying construction?" Lou asked.

"It's awesome," Eli said. "I've done some odd jobs for the Samperis before, when they needed extra crew."

"It's a lot of fun," Shayna agreed. "Yesterday Moss let me run the saw." The way she said it made Lou think Moss had scored another fan.

"The saw's pretty cool, but the real fun is in the finish work. Drywall is an art," Eli said.

"You know how to drywall?" Lou asked. "That's pretty advanced."

"I've done it a couple of times," Eli said, puffing up a little.

"Do you think drywall sounds fun?" Lou asked Shayna.

"I don't know much about it," Shayna admitted.

"Maybe you could show her," Lou suggested.

"Yeah, I guess so," Eli said, sounding a bit shy.

"It doesn't count if you manipulate them into a romance, Cyrano," Benny whispered as he leaned over Lou's shoulder.

"Shoo, fly," Lou said, waving him away.

"You know the Samperis?" Eli asked.

"We go back a ways," Lou said.

"It's so nice they're funding this trip," Shayna said.

"They're not funding it. It's some big corporation," Eli said. "I heard the woman who runs it is a total," he paused with an apologetic glance at Lou, "well, you-know-what."

"Oh, I know," Lou said. "The rumors are true. She's the worst, a total hag."

"You know her, too?" Shayna asked.

"I know everyone," Lou said. "I'm old, and I've been around forever."

"You don't look *that* old," Eli said.

"Wait, didn't Benny say she was on the trip?" Shayna asked.

"Oh, yeah. I didn't see who he was pointing to, did you?" Eli asked.

"No but her name was something unusual, Lou something," Shayna said.

"Lou is a dude's name," Eli agreed.

"Who is she? Is she here?" Shayna asked Lou.

"She only comes out at night. She's kind of a rich eccentric, and she doesn't like the sun," Lou said.

"Why did she come on the trip if she didn't want to work?" Eli asked.

"Rich people are crazy," Lou said.

"What do you do?" Shayna asked her.

"I marry rich men for money," Lou said. "Currently I have my eyes set on Benny Samperi, but I'd be willing to settle for Moss. He seems more easily led, and I'm a woman who likes to be in charge. I'd say you could ask my last two husbands, but they both died in totally explainable and non-mysterious accidents."

They stared at her, blinking. Benny paused by the table again. "Don't believe anything this woman tells you. She's a compulsive liar."

"Mental illness is no joke, Ben," she said.

"I know, Lou. Good to hear you say it, though," he said. "Are you coming, or would you prefer to sit here and torture the children longer?"

"I'm coming," Lou said. "I'll see you guys."

Shayna and Eli didn't reply. It had registered for both of them that Benny called her "Lou." "You blew my cover," she accused. "I was going to try and convince them the mysterious Lou was a vampire."

"You don't have a lot of contact with children, do you?" he asked.

"Children adore fantasy," she said with conviction.

"Eighteen year olds think thirty two year olds who make up stories are insane," he said. "Imagine how we would have felt as kids after a conversation like that."

Lou laughed. "Yeah, I guess I see your point. But in my job, I get so little opportunity to play around. In finance, if you make things up, it usually ends with a prison sentence." She glanced up at him. He didn't seem his usual jolly self. "You're mad at me, huh?"

"Mad, why would I be mad? Men love rejection."

"I didn't reject you. You rejected me."

"I've done nothing but pursue you and you turned me down," he said.

"I didn't turn you down. I turned down your one week limit on us," she said.

"I told you I can't give you more right now," he said.

"I told you I can't accept less right now," she said.

"You're being so stubborn," he said.

"I learned it by watching you," she said. She boarded the bus and sat down. Benny gave the announcements and, when they were finished, went to sit by Molly. Moss boarded the bus, surveyed the scene, and sat beside Lou.

"What's up with you and Benny? He's frowning. I've never actually seen him frown before."

"You'd have to ask him," Lou said. "Are you having a good week so far?"

"Yeah, I guess. I'm basically doing what I normally do, except for no pay," he said, smiling.

"I guess I never thought of it that way. Maybe you should try to do something different, mix it up a little."

"I tried asking Analise if I could help her play doctor. It didn't go over well," he said.

"You might want to stay away from that one," Lou said, tapping her temple.

"That explains why I liked her. I seem incapable of liking nice, normal girls. There's something about the crazy that gets me right here." He thumped his fist over his chest.

"You'll probably grow out of that eventually," she said. "Once your heart gets trampled a few times, you sort of start to decide to do things differently."

"Sounds like you speak from experience," Moss said.

Lou shrugged.

"Well, you couldn't do better than Benny," he continued. "But I'm sure you know that." She didn't respond, but he blustered on, oblivious. "I have to tell you when I first saw you guys together, I didn't get it. We've always joked that Benny will never get married because there will never be another Virgin Mary. But I think we got it all wrong. He doesn't need a saint."

"He needs a sinner?" she guessed.

"No, he needs someone real, someone to bring him down when he's being sanctimonious and to prop him up when he's feeling the weight of the world," Moss said.

"That's incredibly insightful," Lou said.

"It's amazing what you can pick up from playing endless hours of Mario Kart," he said.

Lou glanced outside. Heavy gray clouds began to form. "Hey, Moss, what do we do if it rains?"

"We get wet," he said.

The bus arrived on site, and Benny gathered everyone to speak. "We're going to try and get the roof on today, hopefully before those clouds let loose. Obviously this part isn't for beginners or those afraid of heights. My brothers and I are going to take point up top. Has anyone had roofing experience who feels comfortable going up with us? No pressure. Eli? Good, Eddie, Julia. *Vivian?*"

"I can do it," Vivian insisted.

"She's determined," Giovanni said resignedly.

"All right," Benny said. "Inside team will be working on windows and then I need volunteers to pick up debris on this street to make it more passable."

Lou volunteered to pick up debris. Outside a stiff breeze blew while inside the shelter of the half-constructed building was stifling and stale. Most of the debris was small, so there was much less heavy lifting but a lot more bending and walking. The clouds spit rain off and on throughout the morning. At lunch Lou sat under the tree with Molly. None of the Samperis came down for lunch, so Molly climbed the ladder and carried it up, along with some water. They sat and ate on the roof. Benny glanced down, made eye contact with Lou, and tipped his water to her. She gave him a little salute of approval and got back to work.

After lunch the rain began in earnest. Lou looked around to see if anyone else stopped working; no one else did. She was glad for the cap that kept the drenching rain out of her eyes. And, for the first time in days, she didn't feel so unbearably hot and sweaty. She almost began to feel chilly as the rain soaked through to her skin.

Eventually the rain ended again, and the air became still and humid once more. Lou began to feel truly miserable then, as if she were wading through a swamp. Outside even looked swampy, green and heavy. When the alarm sounded, she had no idea what it was. She had never heard a tornado siren before. It sounded like she had always imagined an air raid siren. Startled, she dropped her load of sticks and covered her ears against the deafening sound.

"Run," someone shouted as she sped past her. Lou turned to see where she was going and saw an underground shelter standing open like a beacon. Volunteers from their group began to pour into it, but for Lou it was like a bad dream. She couldn't run. Her legs and braces wouldn't allow it. So she walked as quickly as she could while everyone else streamed past her. And then Benny was there. He picked her up and put her on his back, piggyback style, and ran them both to the shelter. They descended the steps and the heavy doors were closed. It was dark, silent, and damp in the shelter. Lou realized she was still clinging to Benny like a koala and let go, sliding down the back of him. He grasped her hand and held it tight. Finally someone had the presence of mind to bring out a phone and use a flashlight app.

With the darkness broken, everyone breathed a little easier. Chatter erupted as people began checking their phones.

"It says a funnel cloud was spotted in the other side of the county, moving away from us, and that's what triggered the alarm," Giovanni said, relief palpable in his tone. He put his arm around Vivian and gave her a squeeze. "I had no idea you could slide down a ladder so quickly. If the library doesn't work out, you could be a fireman."

"Fire woman?" she suggested.

"Fire person," he declared.

"A fire person sounds like a villain who shoots fire at people," Moss said. "I would totally do that job."

"Is everyone here?" Benny asked. "Let me do a count."

"Everyone is here, I already counted," Molly said.

Lou opened her mouth to congratulate Molly on her efficiency, but no sound came out. There had been few times in her adult life that her disability had stood in her way, and never had it almost cost her safety.

She wasn't sure if Benny sensed her distress or if he felt distress of his own. Either way, his arm slipped around her and began gently caressing the spot of tension at the base of her neck. Like magic, Lou felt the anxiety begin to drain out of her. She hugged him around the waist. "Thanks."

He kissed her temple. She peered up into his face. They were at the edge of the group in near total darkness. Still, it was an inappropriate place for a private moment. He didn't kiss her, but he wanted to. She could tell by the look on his face. She wanted to kiss him, and he could tell, too. They shared a smile.

"How many times do you think we're going to almost die together?" she whispered.

"Hopefully not as many times as it takes to get it right," he said. His knuckles skimmed along her jawbone.

"You're treading on dangerous ground," she whispered.

"Ever since the moment you plummeted back into my life," he said.

"I've been here all along. You're the one who came back," she said.

"I missed you," he whispered.

"When?" she asked.

"Then, all those years. Today."

"That's revisionist history," she insisted.

"I don't even know what that means," he said.

"You didn't want me then. You made that abundantly clear," she said.

"Lou," he began, but the shelter door above them was yanked open and a police officer stuffed his head inside.

"Y'all okay down there?"

"We're fine, officer," Ben called up. "How's the weather up there?"

"All clear. It was a false alarm. Some suspicious clouds grazed the eastern part of the county and, as you can imagine, we're all a little jumpy here lately when it storms."

"Totally understandable," Benny assured him. He waited, along with Lou, until their entire group emptied from the shelter and then stood behind her to help her up the steep, ladder-like stairs.

"I feel there's a lot of unnecessary touching going on back there," she called to him.

"This is how it's done, trust me," he said. He gave her one last push and they were back in the sunlight, such as it was. "How is everyone feeling? Okay to finish up our projects for the day?"

Everyone assured him they were fine to return to work. He returned to the roof while Lou resumed picking up sticks. They worked for several hours more, until the base structure of the roof was completed, the street was clear, and the windows were in.

This time when they piled back onto the bus, Benny sat with Lou. He picked up her leg and began lifting the hem of her pants.

"What are you doing?" she asked, attempting unsuccessfully to brush him off.

"Satisfying my curiosity about something," he said.

"I'm a mermaid, there I confessed. Now please let go of my pants," she said.

He pushed her pants up and peeked around the edge of one of her braces, gasping slightly as he did so. "Lou, your legs are raw," he whispered. "I wondered after I got a blister on the back of my foot today. How can you stand this?"

"It's not all that unusual. I'll put some medicine on tonight when I take them off. It's fine." She shoved his hands away and pushed down her pants, embarrassed.

"About our earlier conversation," he began, but she interrupted him.

"I don't want to talk about it. The past is the past," she said.

"You don't get to dictate every conversation we have," he said. "I want to talk about it."

"Tough beans," she said.

"Tough beans? What does that even mean?" he asked.

She took a breath. "We're both hungry and tired. Let's please not bicker or discuss anything with the potential to be explosive."

"Reasonable Lou is especially pleasant," he said.

"If we don't get home soon, hungry Lou is going to kill her and eat the body," she said.

He reached into his pocket and pulled out a half-smashed granola bar. "I saved this from lunch." He held it out to her.

She took it as if it were treasure. "I love you," she said, and they froze. "For this," she hastened to add. "I love you for this." She grabbed the granola bar and wolfed it down while he watched in amusement.

"Hey, Lou," he said.

"Hmm." She didn't want to talk now because she had granola breath.

"In case I didn't mention, I'm really glad you're here. I don't know how I would get through this week without you."

"I'm not actually doing that much," she murmured.

"Having someone to lean on is worth more to me than you could possibly know," he said.

"Then by all means, lean on me, chum."

"Did you mean it the friend way that time?" he asked.

"No, but you're getting closer," she said.

"What do I have to do to take it over the line?" he said.

"I can't say for certain, but the granola bar carried you a long way," she said.

"Imagine what I could get with a cheesecake," he said.

"Dare to dream, Samperi," she said.

"Oh, I do, Lou. Believe me, I do."

CHAPTER 18

"Let's talk about prom," Benny said. Supper was finished and they were the last ones at the table.

"I think boutonnieres look ridiculous on anyone but groomsmen, and I don't get the appeal of the YMCA dance. There, I said it," Lou said.

"Let's talk about our prom, the one we didn't go to," he said.

She took his wrist and checked his watch. "It's not go time for that."

"Come on, Lou, we have to talk about it sometime."

"We really don't. Now, if you'll excuse me, I have to go powder my everything."

She stood. He clasped her hand. "Are you coming back?"

"I don't know. I might turn in."

"It's still early. Please come back down. I promise I won't make you talk about anything above the level of a thirteen year old's emotional maturity," he said.

"You promise?" she asked.

"Pinky swear," he said.

When she returned from taking a shower, everyone was in the television room watching a game show. The mood was quiet. Lou guessed exhaustion was beginning to creep in. They'd had early mornings, long days, and endless hours of manual labor. Benny sat on the couch and there were no more seats in the room. He patted his lap and Lou begrudgingly sat on him.

"Did you plan this?" she whispered.

"Yes, everyone in this room is a paid actor. We've been posed this way since you went upstairs," he said.

"Sarcasm is my thing, Samperi. Stay in your lane," she said. His hand rested on her hip and his thumb began to make a slow, gentle circle Lou found immensely soothing. She wasn't aware of falling asleep, but one minute her eyes were open and the next they were closed.

Sometime later, they both woke with a start. The room was dim, the television was off, and the room was empty of people.

"What time is it?" she murmured.

He held his watch to the light. "A little after midnight."

"We slept for three hours, and not one person could tap us on the shoulder as they went by?" she said.

"Maybe they didn't want to disturb us," he said. "We must really have been out."

At some point Lou had shifted sideways so she was curled into him and both his arms were around her. "Your legs must be dead by now."

"You'd think so, but I feel surprisingly comfortable," he said. "Speaking of legs…" He hitched up the hem of her pants, unfastened her braces, pulled them off, and began smoothing his hand up and down her aching calves.

"What are you…that's…okay," she said, closing her eyes again in resigned delight.

"I know your secret," he said.

"That Alfred and I fight crime from our secret lair by night?" she muttered. He was making it hard to think, even of sarcastic comebacks that usually popped to mind so easily.

"That you are incredibly receptive to touch," he said.

"Weirdest comment ever," she mumbled.

"It's kind of a powerful feeling. All I have to do to get you to be quiet is to touch you," he said.

"I bet you say that to all the girls you kidnap and douse with chloroform," she said.

"No, just you, my one and only Lou," he said.

"Remind me to make fun of you more later when I'm not so relaxed," she said. It had been a long time since anyone besides a physical therapist touched her legs, and she didn't think anyone had ever done it with such a heartfelt desire to ease her pain and help her relax. Lou felt like the few minutes he spent gently smoothing his fingers over her were more effective than the last few years of physical therapy combined.

"I know you already have a job, but what are the chances I could hire you to do this forever?" she asked.

"Hire me? I'll do it for free," he said.

She opened her eyes and smiled at him. "What's the quid pro quo, Samperi?" He didn't answer. He simply looked at her. Lou's smile slipped. "Why does it suddenly feel like I have the matches and you have the gasoline?" she whispered.

"Lou, I've been thinking," he whispered, but she held up a hand to stop him.

"Did you hear that?" she asked.

"Are you pretending to have heard something to stop me from speaking?" he asked.

"Shh, listen." Doglike, she cocked her head and strained her ears. A faint giggle sounded from somewhere in the house. Lou refastened her braces and hauled herself off the couch, tugging Benny behind her. They rounded a corner and came face to face with Shayna and Eli, locked in an embrace and kissing frantically in the hallway.

"Hey, y'all," Lou yelled, and the two jumped apart looking guilty. "Watcha guys doing?"

"I, um, she was…" Eli began, looking flushed and more than a little flustered.

"Nothing," Shayna hastened to add. Her eyes narrowed on Benny and Lou. "What were you guys doing?"

"I roam the halls at night looking for someone's essence to steal. It's how I stay young," Lou said. "Benny was helping me find likely candidates. How healthy are you, Shayna?"

Benny put his hand over her mouth. "We were heading to bed. It's kind of late, guys."

Lou pushed his hand away. "You two should not be sneaking out," she blurted.

"We're both eighteen," Shayna said.

"Eighteen? Oh, that's the magical age when you can't get pregnant. Never mind," Lou said.

Eli put his hand over his eyes. "Oh, geez."

"Lou," Benny admonished.

"I'm being real here, Samperi. I intrude because I care," Lou said.

"That's exactly what my mother says," Benny said.

Lou gasped. "You take that back."

"We were only kissing," Shayna said.

"Honey, that's how it starts. Then, nine and a half months later, he's surfing in Mexico while you're trying to push a cantaloupe through a straw. All I'm saying is that kissing is a perfectly acceptable hobby as long as it's taking place during daylight hours and everyone's clothes are firmly in place."

"I've seen you guys kissing twice this week already," Shayna accused.

"That's different," Lou said.

"Why?" Shayna asked.

"Because Benny has malaria, and kissing is the only cure," Lou said.

Now it was Benny's turn to put his hand over his face. "Lou, I am begging you to stop saying things."

"My point is Benny and I are adults with jobs and, should the logical consequences of our behavior occur, we have the resources to handle it, financial or otherwise. You kids are eighteen. You're playing with fire, and your pockets are empty. Go to college, get a job. When you're thirty two, I promise I won't interrupt your kissing sessions with stern warnings," Lou said.

"You're kind of weird," Eli said, but he didn't sound angry.

"Once you reach a certain level of income, it's called eccentric," Lou informed him. "But I care, and I think far too few adults do these days. You both are bright, sensible, and compassionate. I don't want you to stumble into a mistake because you're away from your parents for the first time and you're caught up in a moment. That's what college is for." She snagged Benny's hand. "Now, we are going to go to sleep and trust you two to do the right thing. Good night."

Benny slipped his arm around her shoulders. "Of all my friends, I never would have figured you to turn into a NARC," he said. "You never liked authority."

"I don't think of it as authority; I think of it as guidance. I'm big into mentorship."

"Are you?" he asked, surprised.

She nodded. "My company has a mentorship program for local high school juniors and seniors. We pair them with executives in our firm and bring them in a couple of days a month to work. It's been really successful. So far 98 percent of our kids have gone on to graduate from college. Two of them have been hired by the firm, post graduation."

"Lou, that's amazing. Did you start that?"

"Why do you sound so shocked, Samperi?"

"I don't know. It doesn't gel with my image of you," he said.

"No, you mean it doesn't gel with your image of you. You think you're the only one who cares enough to make a difference, and you think the only way to do it is to kill yourself in some third world country," she said.

"I wouldn't say that," he said.

"Of course you wouldn't," she said. "Your opinion of yourself is way too high."

"Why do you always choose to see the worst in me?" he asked.

"I always choose to see the real you, not the superhero image you wish to portray. And you know what, Samperi? I like the real you, warts and all. I like the man you are better than the man you think you're supposed to be," she said. "You know what my favorite memory of you is?"

"You have one?" he asked.

"Don't pout. My twelfth birthday party, everyone left the pool but us. You edged your way over to me and, with pink cheeks, admitted, 'I can't swim.'"

"What about the part where I rounded everyone up and brought them back to the pool?" he said.

"That was nice, and I appreciated it. But you did stuff like that for everybody. How many people knew you couldn't swim?"

"Only you," he admitted. "You knew all my secrets, all my weaknesses, all my failures."

"And I thought you were the best man in the world anyway," she confessed.

"Until prom," he began.

"Ding, our time is up. Later, Samperi." She stood on her toes, pressed her lips to his, and let herself into her room.

CHAPTER 19

The next morning, Lou went for a swim before the sun came up. The heat was so oppressive it felt like wading through an oven. When she finally came up for air after a long glide, Benny was once again waiting by the side of the pool. He put his hands down and she allowed him to lift her out.

"How do you get out when I'm not here?" he asked. There were no steps into the pool, only ladders.

"I was planning to stay in all day. Forget this mission work nonsense," she said. "What are you doing up so early?"

"Insomnia," he said. His eyes were shadowed. Lou resisted the urge to touch them. They regarded each other in heavy silence.

"I was thinking," he said after awhile. "We made a deal, Lou. We pinky swore you would be my girlfriend, and we each had a stake in the bargain. If you walk away now, you're going to forfeit a whole lot of money when we sign our television contracts."

"Circumstances have changed, and I don't need more money," she said.

"It was never about the money; it was about prestige and bragging rights."

"It's not a good idea to keep on the way we've been. Someone's going to get hurt, most likely me," she said.

"Don't be a welcher," he said.

"Welching is only for betting," she said.

"Fine. I bet we can finish out the week together," he said.

"I had no idea you were this persistent," she said.

"See? We're learning new things about each other; we're growing as a couple," he said.

"What have you learned about me?" she asked.

"That you look so good in a bathing suit, it's worth getting up before sunrise for," he said.

She grinned. "I know it's empty flattery, but I'm going to allow it." Her legs began to wobble. She sank heavily onto a lounger. Benny sat on the lounger beside her, reached for her, and pulled her into his lap.

"For the record, it's not empty flattery. You're doing things to me here, Lou, unexpected, overwhelming and, frankly, terrifying things. I can't seem to keep my mind off you."

"Or your hands," she noted.

"Do you want me to stop touching you?" he asked as one hand gently rubbed the small of her back.

"Maybe later," she said, snuggling closer to him. The sun began to steal over the horizon. They watched it rise together in comfortable silence.

"I don't see much of a future for us," she said a while later.

"Forget the future. Let's focus on the now and take each moment as it comes," he said.

"That's a nice sentiment for a greeting card, but this is real life. My entire career is all about preparing for the future. I'm not sure how to turn it off," she said.

"Don't you think it's worth a try?" he asked. "Come on, Lou, take a chance on me."

"If you start singing ABBA songs, I am out of here," Lou threatened.

"You still haven't given me an answer, Dancing Queen," he said.

"We have three days left on this trip, including today," she noted.

"It's those counting skills that make you a financial whiz," he said.

"I will give you three days, and I will try not to focus on what happens when we get home," she said.

"That's all any fake boyfriend could ask for," he said.

"Tell me, what does a fake couple do on the fourth day of their fake relationship?" she asked.

"I have no idea. It's been a long time. If we were Giovanni and Vivian, we'd be married by now."

"I don't think we're there yet. Maybe tomorrow."

"Something to look forward to," he said. "I guess we should go to breakfast and get this day started."

"Go time?" she asked.

"Go time," he said. He reached for her braces and fastened them for her before helping her stand. Inside she went upstairs to shower while he went in search of coffee.

CHAPTER 20

The next day, someone knocked on Lou and Molly's door while it was still dark outside. "It's five in the morning," Lou complained. "It had better not be go time already."

Molly sprang out of bed and opened the door. Moss stood on the other side. "Lou, Benny's sick," he said. His tone sent a flutter of panic through Lou's midsection. She sat up and reached for her braces. "You have to come *now*," Moss added.

"Give her a minute," Molly snapped, surprising all of them.

Lou fastened her braces in record time, grabbed her robe, and climbed out of bed. She and Molly followed Moss down the stairs, albeit not as rapidly as he would have liked. "This is as fast as I can go, unless you'd like to carry me on your back like a mama possum," Lou explained after Moss gave her the fourth impatient glance in a row. At last they reached Benny and Moss's room and went inside.

As soon as they entered the room, Lou could tell it was bad. He was out of his mind with fever, drenched with sweat, and making a sound halfway between a moan and a mutter.

"Molly, call Analise and then you're in charge for today. Moss, bring water, juice, tea, basically any liquids you can find. And grab me a cool washcloth from the bathroom," she directed. She sat beside

Benny, pulled back the covers that were twisted around him, and pressed her hand to his forehead. It was raging with fever.

"Benny," she said softly.

He opened his eyes. Even in the soft light from the nightstand, they looked sunken, glazed, and yellow. "Lou. How did you get past my mom?" he mumbled.

She would laugh, if the situation weren't so dire. Moss handed her the washcloth and she began to smooth it over Benny's forehead and chest. He sighed roughly as if torn between relief and pain.

Moss returned with an armful of various liquids. Lou opened an apple juice, inserted a straw, and plunged it between Benny's lips with an order to drink. He did so, sputtering a little when the liquid hit his throat. After the initial swallow, he sucked the rest down greedily, as if he had never tasted liquid before. When the first container was finished, Lou switched to a glass of sweet tea. He guzzled half of it before finally laying back down again, his breathing slightly less ragged. She sponged his face, arms, and chest again with the cloth and then, about ten minutes later, gave him a few more sips to drink.

She repeated the process until Analise arrived, winded and with her hair in a messy topknot that looked more cute than hurried. Even without makeup the girl was a beauty, and Lou stamped down an unhealthy stab of envy. Lou was the type of woman who felt her appearance needed immaculate attention. She had never been able to pull off a makeup-free messy bun, and she doubted she ever would. Her only consolation was that Benny had seen her without makeup plenty of times, and he never seemed to mind.

Analise took his temperature and pulse and listened to his heart and lungs. "His fever's almost 104," she commented.

"I think that's down," Lou said. "He was delirious when I got here."

"Everything else seems all right. He needs rest and fluids. I'll stay with him today," Analise said.

"I'll stay," Lou said.

"We don't both need to stay," Analise said. "And I'm a doctor."

"If he needs you, I'll call again. Thanks for coming, but I'm sure you have better things to do today," Lou said.

"He has a precarious medical condition. I think I should be the one to stay," Analise said.

"I think if we woke him and asked him which of us he wanted to stay, we both know the answer would be me. Again, thank you for coming, I really appreciate it. Stop by later to check on him, if you like. I'll be here all day."

They stared each other down until at last Analise began angrily tossing things into her bag. When she finished, she stalked out of the room without another word.

"She really is crazier than a bag of cats," Moss said. "I think I might love her."

"Make sure to get a pre-nup," Lou commented before turning her attention back to Benny who continued to rest and breathe comfortably now.

"Do you need anything before I go?" Moss asked.

"I'm good, and I'm sure Sheila would be willing to send anything I need," Lou said. After initially making fun of their over-eager hostess, she had come to enjoy her over-the-top southern persona. Hospitality was key in Sheila's world, and Lou was old enough to realize what a rare gift that was.

"I'll have my phone, so call me or Giovanni or Vivian if anything changes," Moss said.

"We'll be fine," Lou assured him.

Moss remained by the door, watching his brother. "It's hard to see him like this."

"He's going to be all right," Lou assured him. "He's strong."

"Until the next time he goes to some forsaken country without proper medical care," Moss said. They made eye contact until Lou looked away. How could she comfort him when she'd had the same thought? "At least he's in good hands for today. See you, and thanks, Lou."

"Thanks for coming to get me," Lou said.

"He asked for you," Moss said. "That was what woke me up."

When he was gone, Lou shucked off her braces and crawled into the bed beside Benny. He didn't stir. She lay looking at him a long time, until it was time for him to drink more again. When she was satisfied he was properly hydrated, she fell asleep.

He was looking at her, when she woke a couple of hours later. "How are you feeling?" she asked.

"Like I fell off the malaria wagon, and then it backed up and ran over me," he said.

She reached to the nightstand on the other side of him and gave him something else to drink.

"This is torture," he croaked.

"I know, but you have to drink," she said.

"No, I mean the fact you're in my bed wearing a silky black nighty, and I'm too sick and weak to do anything about it," he said. When the drink was finished, he closed his eyes and fell back asleep.

Fully awake now, Lou reached for the remote. She turned on the television and muted it, despite the fact that a foghorn probably wouldn't be able to wake Benny at this point. A couple of hours later, he woke again. She helped him to the bathroom and waited outside the door.

"Are you all right in there?" she called when he seemed to be taking a long time.

"I'm brushing my teeth," he said, or at least that was what she thought he said. It sounded more like, "Ahm bushing ma feef." He emerged pale and shaking and she helped him hobble back to bed.

"You know you're in bad shape when you're relying on the handicapped person to help you walk," she said, and he laughed weakly before she shoved another strawful of water into his mouth. "Do you want something to eat?"

He nodded. She opened a packet of crackers from the nightstand and gave him one. "What are you watching?" he asked as he munched.

"I have no idea. I haven't watched television in forever. Good to know I haven't missed anything. Do you know this is my first vacation in five years?" she said.

"What did you do the last time you took a vacation? Sit with someone who had typhoid fever?" he asked.

"I went to homecoming at Princeton with some friends. It was our five year college reunion and we went to the football game," she said.

"Sounds fun," he said.

"It was a blast," she agreed. "You should co—You should go to a Princeton game sometime. They're fun."

"I'd like that," he said. "Can I see your phone?"

She handed him the phone. He held it in the air above them. "Malaria selfie," he said, and snapped a photo. For the next few minutes, he busied himself scrolling through the pictures on her phone. She didn't think much of it until he spoke again.

"Who's this?" He turned the phone toward her to show a picture of her on the beach, being held aloft by a man.

"That's Zel," she said.

"What's a Zel?" he asked.

"Good question," she said and turned toward the TV again.

He put his hand on her arm. "Lou, who is Zel?"

"He was my fiancé," she said and Benny almost dropped the phone.

"You were engaged?" he asked.

"Operative word being were," she said.

"When was this?" he asked.

"After college," she said. "We were college sweethearts."

"What happened?" he asked.

"He decided he'd rather be post-college sweethearts with my best friend. I found them together two weeks before our wedding." She turned up the television.

Benny stared at the picture a few minutes before tossing it onto the nightstand. "Well, that sucks."

"It did, yes," she agreed. "I'm over it now."

"His picture on your phone says otherwise."

"It's a good picture of me, I look hot," she said.

He picked up the phone and studied the picture again. "True, but you always look that way."

She scowled at him. "I haven't seen a mirror today, but I'm fairly certain there's a rat's nest in my hair, so you're pretty much lying."

"Honey, you're wearing a black, silk nightie. As far as I'm concerned at this moment, you don't even have hair," he said.

She laughed and resumed her focus on the television. Benny picked up the remote and clicked it off. "Hey, I was watching *Judge Judy*," she complained.

"Let's talk about prom," he said.

"No." She started to get out of bed, but he rolled on top of her.

"Look who made a miraculous recovery," she said.

"This is all I've got, and I lack the strength to roll back off of you, so you might as well listen. You think I stood you up for prom."

"You did, in fact, stand me up for prom," she said.

"Okay, I did, and it was a total jerk move. But it wasn't for the reason you thought," he said.

"I know why it was; it was because you didn't want to go to prom with the girl in the chair," she said.

"If I didn't want to go to prom with the girl in the chair, why did I ask the girl in the chair to prom?" he said.

That gave her pause. "Pity?"

He snorted a laugh. "I have never pitied you, Lou. I've pitied the people who have gotten in your way, and I pitied those kids you mortified away from ever kissing again, but my pity has never extended to you."

She sighed. "Fine, I'll ask the question you want me to ask. Why did you stand me up for prom?"

"Because it all seemed to be leading somewhere. Our friendship was changing, and I didn't know how to deal with it."

"You could have told me straight up you didn't want to be with me," she said.

"See, this is where you got it wrong. I did want to be with you, Lou. I convinced myself we were in love."

She paused, letting the weight of that sink in. "Then why?" she whispered.

"Because I knew we had no future. I knew you were staying put and I was going away, and I didn't want to lose our friendship. It seemed like a no-win situation. So I thought if we didn't go to prom, nothing would change. We wouldn't have some big, romantic night pushing us over the edge."

"You broke my heart, Ben," she said. "I dropped out of school, I *fled the country* because of you."

"I'm sorry," he said. "You have no idea how sorry, Lou. I wrote you a million letters, but I could never say the right thing, and I didn't know where you were to send them. I convinced myself it was better that way, that it was inevitable we would be separated eventually and the break would hurt less if I let things go. I'm deeply and desperately sorry. Will you please forgive me?" His eyes were misty, and Lou felt her own eyes well with tears.

"Yes," she whispered, and he kissed her. It was a different sort of kiss, one that touched a place in Lou's heart so deep she hadn't opened it to him before. Maybe she hadn't opened it to anyone before, maybe it had been waiting for him. It felt as if time had been stripped away and they were sharing the kiss they should have shared all those years ago as love-struck seventeen year olds. All the old love and adoration she'd held for him came rushing to the surface, and she clung to him, wanting the kiss to go on forever.

Benny seemed to want the same thing, and it might have happened, if they hadn't been interrupted.

"Well, this looks nice and cozy," Benny's mother said. She stood in the center of the room, her arms loaded down with a basket of food.

CHAPTER 21

"Ma!" Benny exclaimed. He flopped onto his back and away from Lou like a fish that had been shot with a spear.

"Did another one of my sons go and get secretly married?" Mrs. Samperi asked.

"No one's married, Ma," Benny said. "What are you doing here?"

"Moss told me you were sick. By the amount of hanky-panky going on, I see you're feeling much better," Mrs. Samperi said. "Hello, Lou. It's nice to see you, and so very much of you all at once."

Blushing, Lou pulled the blankets up to her neck. "There was no hanky-panky, Mrs. Samperi. Just a little hanky."

"Well, let's put the panky away until after the wedding, all right?" Mrs. Samperi said. Unlike her children, she had a thick Brooklyn accent that made everything she said a little bit scarier and more commanding. Still, Lou had always liked her, and she laughed through her embarrassment.

"Please tell me I'm having another delusion," Benny said, his hand over his eyes.

"It's all too real, son. Put some pants on and eat your food." She set a basket on the bed and began unloading it.

"I bet that's not the first time you've had to say that to one of your children," Lou said, and Mrs. Samperi shook her head.

"Lou, honey, you have no idea. Motherhood is not easy. Keep that in mind as you go forward because, at the rate it looked like you two were headed, you'll find out soon enough."

Benny groaned again and Lou covered her mouth to choke back a laugh. "Ma," Benny groaned. "I'm thirty two."

"A mother stops being a mother because her children grow up?" Mrs. Samperi said, sounding wounded.

"Benny, how could you treat your mother so poorly?" Lou asked, poking him.

His gaze slid to her, astounded. "Are you actually taking her side after she burst in here unannounced and without knocking and then embarrassed us like we're a couple of teenagers?"

"Don't forget I cooked all your favorite foods all morning and drove breakneck speed more than two hours to get here," Mrs. Samperi said.

"Benny, for shame," Lou said.

Benny put up his hand. "I can't even, with you two. It's like when Godzilla teamed up with King Kong."

Mrs. Samperi tossed Lou one of Benny's shirts. "I always liked you, Lou. Put this on and have some food." She arranged food while Lou and Benny put on the requisite clothing and then handed them heaping plates when they were finished.

"Where'd you go to, Lou? You dropped out of our lives without a word."

"After your son stood me up for prom, I took a year to see the world," Lou said.

Mrs. Samperi's eyes flew to her second born. "He did what?"

"Tell her, Benny," Lou prodded.

"I faked being sick and stood Lou up for prom," Benny said in the tone of a repentant five year old.

Mrs. Samperi began sorting through her basket. "Where's my spoon?"

"You can't spank me, Ma. The statute of limitations has expired," Benny said.

"I can and I will, as soon as I find my spoon. You apologize to Lou."

"That's what I was doing when you interrupted us," Benny said.

"Oh, in that case, it looked like you did a thorough job of it. Maybe too thorough. How are your parents, Lou?"

Lou couldn't answer until she stopped laughing. "They're doing well, keeping busy."

"I imagine they are, with a foundation to run," Mrs. Samperi said.

"What foundation?" Benny asked.

"The Hartwell Foundation. It's a charity Lou and her parents started when her father retired. Though he keeps so busy running the foundation I'm not sure it can be called retirement," Mrs. Samperi said.

Benny almost dropped his plate. He stared at Lou, openmouthed. She, meanwhile, studiously avoided his gaze.

"What's with the fish face, son?" Mrs. Samperi said, noting Benny's gaping lips.

"For years one of my main donors has been the Hartwell Foundation," he said. "I had no idea it was the Lawtons. How could you not have told me that, Lou?"

"You never asked," Lou said.

"What was I supposed to say? Have you secretly been funding my life for the last half decade while I thought you hated me?"

"I told you I didn't hate you, and somebody had to do it. Globe trotting doesn't come cheap," she said.

"I can't believe you. My entire life has been turned upside down at this revelation, and you sit there calmly eating spaghetti," he said.

"That's angel hair, son," Mrs. Samperi interjected. "You're Italian, for goodness sake, learn the difference."

"Don't be so dramatic, Benny," Lou said.

"He's always been a little bit of a drama king," Mrs. Samperi agreed.

Benny waved his hand between them. "No, you two are not allowed to team up against me. No, nope, stop it."

"See? Drama king," Mrs. Samperi said while Lou nodded her agreement.

"This is like a nightmare," Benny said. A knock sounded at the door. "Who could that be? My grandmother, come to throw her two cents into the ring? Her priest? A proctologist reminding me of my annual checkup?" But, no, it was Giovanni, Moss, and Vivian.

"We smelled food. Oh, and we wanted to check on you," Giovanni said. He entered and began filling a plate from the overflowing containers. His mother always brought enough to feed a regiment.

"Moss, you tattled to Mom I was sick," Benny accused.

"She dragged it out of me," Moss defended, his cheeks stuffed with alfredo.

"Let me guess, she said, 'hi,'" Giovanni said.

"What's wrong with your mother knowing you're sick?" Mrs. Samperi asked. "Families shouldn't keep secrets. That's right, I'm looking at you, Giovanni and Vivian."

"Lou's wearing Benny's shirt and no pants, and Benny's wearing pants and no shirt. You're like the real life Mickey and Minnie Mouse," Moss said.

"It's exactly like that episode where Mickey got malaria," Giovanni said.

Lou had forgotten how loud the Samperis were when they got together. Her ears felt bruised, but she loved it. It was a fun, drastic departure from being an only child.

"Someone text Molly to come up," Mrs. Samperi said.

"I thought it was family only," Moss said.

"No, we're doing it by how much we like people. Time for you to go, Moss," Giovanni said.

"Boys," Mrs. Samperi scolded. "Benny, remind your brothers to love each other. Family is forever."

Benny gave Lou an apologetic glance. *I'm so sorry,* he mouthed.

"This is not my first ride on the Samperi carousel," she reminded him. "I'm enjoying it. It feels like old times."

"So," Mrs. Samperi said, clapping her hands together. "Who is going to be the first one to give me a grandchild? Vivian, Lou, we have an actual horse race now, and the clock is ticking. Although, Lou, I insist you be married first."

"What about Peaches?" Lou asked after she stopped choking. The room grew suddenly quiet.

"Peaches is, well, we don't talk about it," Mrs. Samperi said, her tone heavy. "So it's between you two. A pregnancy announcement can be my birthday gift this year."

"But we're not…" Lou began, but Benny rested his hand on her leg and shook his head. "Don't engage. It'll go worse for you. Smile and nod. See, Vivian's learned." He pointed to his sister-in-law who was smiling and nodding like a deranged bobble head.

Lou imitated her, grinning wildly and dipping her head.

"Good. I'd prefer a boy first. Everyone should have an older brother," Mrs. Samperi said. "Who's still hungry? There's more food."

Molly arrived then, and conversation turned to a recounting of the day's activities. Supper came to an end, and Mrs. Samperi began to gather her food.

"Now girls, remember what I said. My birthday is three months away. Lou, that's going to be pushing it to sneak in a wedding and a pregnancy, but I'm not pressuring you to put the cart before the horse. Remember that."

"I will remember this conversation forever," Lou assured her.

"Good. Now, boys, about your part in things. When your father and I…"

"No," Benny exclaimed, and the three brothers looked like the see no evil, hear no evil, speak no evil monkeys as Benny covered his eyes, Giovanni put his hands over his ears, and Moss pressed his palm to his mouth.

"Ma, do not ever finish that sentence, I am begging you," Giovanni said.

"I was going to say when your father and I were dating, he always brought flowers. He was romantic and attentive, as I hope you boys are to your ladies," she said, and a general sigh of relief went around the room.

"And of course he's very fertile, as proved by you five, so I don't think you'll have any problems in that department," Mrs. Samperi added.

"I, for one, had no worries," Moss said with a wink at Molly no one else in the room besides her saw.

"My fertility has lowered fifteen percent since this conversation began," Giovanni declared.

Vivian and Lou remained perfectly still and silent, as if trying not to attract attention and restart the uncomfortable conversation.

Soon after that, everyone began to drift away, first Mrs. Samperi, and then those who had shown up for her food. Eventually only Lou and Benny were left. Benny lay back on the bed with a sigh.

"Sweet freedom. I swear Peaches and Vivian should qualify for sainthood for voluntarily joining this family."

"Are Peaches and Joe not together anymore? Because I could never believe in true love again if those two ever broke up," Lou said.

"They're still together, it's…all couples go through stuff sometimes, I guess."

Lou lay back, too. "That was the first time I've ever been directly in your mom's targets. It's kind of terrifying."

"Like standing in front of a fire hose filled with crazy," Benny said. "Are you having second thoughts?"

"About what? It's only one more day," she reminded him.

"One more day, right." He propped himself on one elbow. "What other secrets are you hiding from me, Lou? Today I found out you had a fiancé, a canceled wedding, and you've been secretly financially supporting my life for years. Are you a double agent? CIA assassin?"

"What about you? I discovered a pretty big secret of my own. I thought you didn't want me all those years ago, and it turns out my crush was mutual," she said. "Mind blown."

"Oh, it was more than a crush," he said.

"Yeah? How much more?" she asked.

"I carved our initials in a tree," he said.

"Which tree?"

"An oak tree on my parents' property. I needed an outlet, and I had no one else to tell because the person I told everything to was you," he said. "And then there's this." He reached for his wallet, rifled through a stack, and handed her a small, dog-eared photograph.

"It's us," she exclaimed. "When was this? I don't remember it."

"Joe took it when he was going through that big photography phase. I think we were about fifteen and working on some project at my house," he said.

"Have you really kept this in your wallet all these years, or did you stuff this in here last week when you knew I'd be coming on the trip?" she asked.

"So suspicious, Hattie Lou," he said. "Is it too much to believe a guy carries around a picture of the first girl he ever loved?"

"Benny," she said, exasperated.

"What?"

"When I lose all faith in humanity, you reel me in again," she said.

"It's what I do," he said. He lay down again and they spent some time looking at each other.

"It's weird to look at you," she noted after a while.

"Thank you?" he said.

"I see the boy and the man. Pre-muscled teenager kind of morphs together with this guy," she touched her fingers to his chest.

"Pre-muscled teenager has a lot in common with post-malaria thirty-two year old," he said. "I feel like I lost about a third of my body weight, although my mom has been doing her best to put it back on me."

"I have zero complaints," Lou said. She leaned forward and pressed her lips to his jaw.

He drew her closer and kissed her in earnest. It was a different sort of kiss for both of them. Throughout the day, something had shifted. Neither of them could put a name to it, but both of them felt it. It was less a frenzied kiss of attraction and more a tender kiss of longing and affection. Something in Lou's heart pinged dangerously, and she pulled away.

"I should go. I haven't showered since last night, and I've been wearing this nightie for twenty four hours," she said.

"That's exactly what I was thinking. Please go, ick." He drew her impossibly closer and pressed his face to her neck. "Don't go."

"This is not going to end well," she said.

"Don't think about the end," he admonished.

"You're right, I'm trying. But I do have to go. I feel grimy."

"Okay," he said, but he made no move to let her go. She was cinched tightly in his embrace and his face was still pressed to her neck. Eventually she realized he had fallen asleep. She stayed until Moss came into the room, then she eased out of Benny's embrace, pressed a kiss to his head, and let herself out.

CHAPTER 22

The next morning, in the soft gray of early daylight, Molly O'Ryan woke to see Lou standing over her bed, fully dressed and wide awake.

"It's the last day of camp and time for pranks. Are you in?"

Molly blinked, trying to orient her brain. "Yes."

"Good, let's text Vivian. Something tells me she's going to want to get in on this."

Later, downstairs, Moss and Benny saw Giovanni sitting alone at a table, his nose stuck in a book.

"Where are the women?" Moss asked him.

"I've been waiting to read this book for four months, so basically a nuclear bomb could detonate and I'd have no idea," Giovanni said.

"How can you read that? There are no pictures," Moss said.

Giovanni set down the book. "Are you purposely trying to imitate Gaston from *Beauty and the Beast,* or are you genuinely ignorant?"

"Dude, why do you know *Beauty and the Beast* so well?" Moss said.

"I'm married to a library loving brunette who sings. You do the math," Giovanni said.

"You can't walk away when she's watching? Time to pull out the man card and assert yourself, son," Moss said.

"Oh, Moss, you poor, poor idiot. Do you know what the man card is good for after you're married? Framing, so you can look at it and say, 'I remember when that used to work,'" Giovanni said.

"Dude, I am never getting married," Moss said.

"The women of the world just rejoiced, and they have no idea why," Benny said.

"Seriously, though, do you always have to give in after you're married?" Moss asked.

"It's not giving in if you get something in return," Giovanni said.

"What do you get in return?" Moss asked.

Giovanni picked up his book and resumed reading, smiling.

"I don't get it," Moss said.

"Sex, Moss, he's talking about sex," Benny said, a little too loudly because a few people at surrounding tables turned to look at them. Benny gave them a sheepish wave.

"If you have to watch *Beauty and the Beast* to get sex, you're doing it wrong, am I right?" Moss said and held up his fist to Benny for a bump.

"How would I know?" Benny asked, ignoring the bump. "Last time I made a move on a woman, Mom showed up."

"Get used to it because she'll keep doing it," Giovanni said.

"You're joking," Benny said.

"Oh, I wish I were. A few weeks ago, Vivian and I, well, let's say we were enjoying a good showing of *Beauty and the Beast,* when there was a knock at the door. Of course we knew it was Ma, so we pretended not to be home."

"Did that work?" Moss asked.

"Yes, Moss, it worked perfectly and we all lived happily ever after, that's why I'm telling you this story," Giovanni said. "Of course it didn't work, it's Ma. She let herself in with the secret key I didn't know she had made, came up to our bedroom, knocked on the door, and yelled, 'Did you change out your flannel sheets? I need to know because I wash those on a different setting.'"

"Oh, man," Benny said. "What did Vivian do?"

Giovanni smiled. "Vivian continued to pretend nobody was home, bless her. I love that woman. That's what you have to do with Ma, pretend like she's not there, spewing crazy into your life."

"I'm pretty sure Lou could match her, crazy for crazy," Benny said.

"Now there's a competition I'd pay to see," Giovanni said.

"Yeah, today's the last day, though," Benny said.

"Last day of what?" Moss asked because Giovanni was once again engrossed in his book.

"Last day for me and Lou."

"Why?" Moss asked.

"It's a long story, but suffice it to say we don't have much of a future together after this week," Benny said.

"Why?" Moss asked.

"Because she's staying here, and I'm not," Benny said.

"Why?" Moss asked.

"Because it's time for me to get back to my real life and my real job," Benny said.

"Why?" Moss asked.

"Moss," Giovanni exclaimed, setting down his book with a thump. "Learn another word."

"Why?" Moss asked, grinning as only a youngest child can.

"I swear, we're all going to take up a collection and get Molly therapy for her interest in you," Giovanni said, and Moss's smile changed to a frown.

"I am a catch," Moss said.

"So was malaria," Benny informed him. He scanned the room. "Where are the women?"

"I don't know, but my spidey sense is tingling," Moss said.

"That's your brain trying to function. It's an unfamiliar sensation, but nothing to fear," Giovanni said.

"Uh, maybe we should compare SAT scores, genius," Moss said.

"You didn't take the SAT, you took the ACT, *genius*" Giovanni said.

"Oh, never mind. Unless it's like golf, where a low score is good," Moss said.

"You suck at golf, too," Giovanni said.

"It's so boring," Moss whined.

Giovanni gave him his book. "Here, try to sound out some of the words while the grownups talk. Pro-tip: t-h-e is *the*."

"I'm telling Mom when we get home, and you are in so much trouble," Moss said.

"The fact that I'm not sure if you're joking is the saddest part of this conversation," Giovanni said.

Benny tuned out their bickering, as he always did. Being the two youngest, only three years apart, and polar opposites had set them at odds since Moss's birth. Giovanni had always been a saver, of both money and candy, while Moss had always spent money as soon as he got it and ate his candy immediately until he threw up. Then he would beg Giovanni to "borrow" some of his, and the cycle would repeat until the next holiday. Giovanni was more mature and easier to take for long periods of time, but Moss was still lovable and sweet, when he wasn't doing his level best to get under everyone's skin on purpose. In a family of five kids, he had thrived by being the pest no one could stand to have around for long, except their mother who never grew tired of his immaturity or bad decisions. In fact, the family was convinced she preferred him that way. His poor life choices left a lot of cleaning up for her to do. She was never not busy when Moss was around and, since he still lived at home, he was always around.

Beneath Benny's annoyance at his youngest brother was a flicker of worry. Moss's shtick had been cute when he was little, but he was twenty five now and everyone's patience with him was growing thin, most notably their father's. Pete Samperi believed retirement should include more freedom and travel with his wife. Marie Samperi had other ideas—since Moss wasn't ready to leave the nest, she saw no need to push him out. Benny hoped Moss would grow up and move out on his own before everything came to a head. His brother had the basics he needed to thrive, if only he could pull himself together and act like a man instead of a little boy.

"I'm going to text Molly and see where they are," Moss said, pulling Benny back to the present.

"I'll text," said Giovanni. He pulled out his phone and sent a text to his wife.

They're getting suspicious, better hurry, Vivian read when she received Giovanni's text.

"Time to clear the room," she said to Lou and Molly, who finished screwing in the showerhead after dumping a few packets of Kool-Aid inside.

"Are we sure we're done here?" Lou asked.

"Saran Wrap on toilets, underwear stolen, shoes tied together, socks dunked in water and put back in the bag, sheets shorted, and fake snakes and spiders hidden in beds. I think we got everything," Molly said, checking her list. "This is so exciting. I've never pranked anyone before."

"And I've never seen anyone make an organized checklist for pranking before," Lou said. "I'd make fun of you, but I wholeheartedly approve your methods."

"And I wholeheartedly approve you packing prank supplies in anticipation of this day," Vivian said. "It didn't even occur to me to be mean-spirited this week."

Lou tapped her temple. "It's always on the forefront of my brain. Are you going to do anything to Giovanni?"

"Are you joking? Giovanni got a pen mark on his favorite pair of chinos and spent two days watching stain removal videos on YouTube until he was certain he had enough training to remove it," Vivian said. "Pranking him would make my life miserable. Besides, it's way more fun to prank my brothers-in-law."

"It's not brother-in-laws?" Molly asked.

"Never bring a clipboard to a grammar fight with a librarian," Lou said.

"She's right," Vivian agreed. "Two things I never joke about are grammar, tacos, and counting."

"They kind of look like a team now, don't they?" Benny asked as the women entered the room, laughing.

"Yeah, do you think they were talking about us?" Moss asked, the suspicion in his tone matching that of Benny's.

"I'm reading my book," Giovanni said and put his book up to his face.

"What have you ladies been up to?" Moss asked as the women approached and sat down.

"Recalibrating the sphignometer," Lou said.

"What?" Moss asked, squinting in confusion.

"Rebonics of the capacitator," Lou said.

"Huh?" Moss tried.

"Alakabazim flaptater," Lou replied and Moss gave up, shaking his head as if trying to clear water from his ears. Ben, however, was now regarding her with no small amount of suspicion.

"You used to use that tactic on the athletes when you'd done something rotten in school," he said. "Where have you been?" He held up a finger. "Keep in mind speaking gibberish won't work on me."

"Naked," she replied, and he completely lost the flow of the conversation.

"What were we talking about?" he said after a minute of staring at his plate in consternation.

She shrugged and turned to roll her eyes at Molly and Vivian. Moss, who was sitting close to Molly, leaned in to whisper in her ear.

"Mol, what's your favorite Disney cartoon?"

Now it was her turn to be confused. "*Enchanted*," she replied, but it came out sounding like a question. "Why?"

"Future reference," he said, and chucked her under the chin.

CHAPTER 23

The final day was spent in a blitz of work. They finished the building they had been working on, but there was no time to admire it because there was always something else to do. The streets around the building had been cleared of debris, and the Samperis poured a foundation for the next building that would be rebuilt by another team the following week.

That evening Sheila had planned a crab boil for them. The atmosphere was festive, but Lou sat on Benny's lap in a lawn chair at the far side of the fire, watching instead of taking part.

"I should be mingling," Benny said, his voice close to Lou's ear.

"You are, you're mingling with me," she said.

"I should be talking with everyone," he said.

"You're exhausted," she pointed out.

"I'm exhausted," he agreed.

"You overdid today," she said.

"I overdid today," he admitted.

She turned her head slightly and peered up at him. "What else can I get away with making you say?"

"How about 'I don't want today to be the last day,'" he suggested.

"I don't want today to be the last day," Lou said.

"Me, neither," he said and touched his lips to hers.

She closed her eyes and savored the light kiss, wondering how many more there would be.

"Are you cold?" he asked.

She shook her head.

"You have goose bumps," he pointed out, his finger skimming down her arm.

"That's how my pores exercise," she said.

"Oh, I thought it was a reaction to me and my kisses," he said.

"Don't flatter yourself. My follicles are extremely health conscious," she said. She closed her eyes again as his fingers continued to trail down her arms, sending her nerve endings into overdrive.

"They're going to overexert," he said, referencing the hairs on her arms still standing at attention.

"I think they might be mentally ill," she said.

"They're not alone," he said, his lips nibbling the rim of her ear.

"You're killing me here," she said. No one could see what he was doing to her in the semi-darkness on the lawn, but her boneless response to him was on full display.

"Who killed Lou?" Moss asked as he came to claim the empty lawn chair beside them, Molly in his wake.

"She had too much to drink," Benny explained.

"There's no alcohol here," Moss said.

"She carries a flask," Benny said.

"That kind of explains a lot," Moss said.

"Doesn't it, though?" Benny agreed.

"I am neither dead nor deaf," Lou said, reluctantly pulling herself to an upright position away from Benny. "And I'm not drunk."

"That's what drunk people always say," Moss said. "Say your ABC's backwards while walking a line and touching your nose."

"You first," Lou said.

"He can't do that sober," Giovanni said as he and Vivian joined the group.

"I am so bored," Moss announced. "Someone entertain me."

"Does anyone have one of those little mirrors Moss could stare into for a while?" Giovanni asked.

"Let's do something," Lou agreed.

"Listen to the drunky," Moss urged. He tipped his hand up and made a "glug, glug" sound.

She smacked him on the arm. "I am not drunk, you miscreant."

"Oh, Lou, you can't use big words on Moss. That's how he broke his brain the first time," Giovanni said.

"Let's go swimming," Lou suggested and Benny groaned.

"The pool's all crowded, and Analise is in there," Molly said, her nose wrinkling in distaste.

"Let's go swimming in the lake," Lou said.

"With, like, fish and snakes and turtles and stuff?" Moss asked uncertainly.

"No, I asked that those be removed upon our arrival," Lou said. He nodded, frowning thoughtfully. "Come on, you guys, you've never swum in a lake at night before?"

"I think it sounds like a blast," Vivian said.

"I'm in," Molly said.

"It feels wrong when you three collude," Benny said.

"I don't know, I don't like vermin," Moss said.

"Vermin are rod…you know what, I'm too tired," Giovanni said.

"Come on, Moss. You said you live for adventure. Was that all talk?" Molly goaded.

"I meant like skydiving and racecar driving. Not eels and snakes and junk," Moss said.

"Giovanni's in," Vivian announced.

"Why am I in?" he asked.

"Because we're married," she replied.

"You already used that one today when you wanted me to get up and get you more mustard," Giovanni said.

She tapped her ring. "That's why you should always read the contract, baby, it never expires."

"Stupid eternal vows. Looks like I'm in," he said.

"And Benny's in, obviously," Lou added.

"I don't even like to swim in the pool. What makes you think I'm game for swimming in a darkened lake?" Benny asked.

"Because we're still in that phase of the relationship where you're trying to impress me and earn my love," Lou said.

"Why does it feel like we've been in that phase since we were twelve?" he asked.

"That only leaves Moss, but maybe he's too chicken," Lou said.

"Maybe I could sit on the bank and talk to you guys while you swim," Moss suggested.

"Bock," Lou said.

"I'm not chicken," Moss.

"Bock, bock," Molly added.

"Molly, you too?" Moss asked.

And then everyone started clucking and flapping until he eventually relented. They changed into their swim clothes and met back at the lake.

"Hey, those were some delightful pranks you left in our room," Benny said, picking Lou up by the waist and spinning her in a circle.

"I don't know what you're talking about, but it was probably Sheila. Her charming southern demeanor is a cover for her psychopathic tendencies," Lou said.

"Sounds like most southern women I know," Moss added. "In Brooklyn, no one tries to hide their crazy with sweet tea and monograms."

Lou took off her braces and she and Benny dashed into the water, diving deep and swimming far out. Giovanni and Vivian came next, albeit more tentatively. At last it was only Moss and Molly left on the shore.

"The animals are more scared of you than you are of them," Molly said.

"I really doubt that," Moss said, daring to stick one toe into the water.

"Come on, Moss," Molly coaxed, holding out her hand to him. "If you're brave, I'll give you a treat."

He took her hand. "What kind of a treat?"

"I have a sucker in my purse," she said.

"What makes you think I want food, Molly?" he asked and then reversed roles by running into the water and tugging her along behind him.

They paired off and swam for a while and then came back together as a group, albeit spaced widely apart.

"I think we should take it up a notch," Lou said.

"Do you want me to toss some electric wires into the lake, see if we can dodge them?" Benny asked.

"No, I think we should skinny dip," Lou said.

"What?" Giovanni replied.

"Done," Vivian said, holding her suit aloft.

He turned to her in astonishment. "Woman, you're *nekked*!"

"It's all right, Giovanni, we're married," Vivian reminded him.

"We're not married to everyone here. I would prefer my brothers not see what I get to see in the privacy of our home," Giovanni said.

"It's too dark to see anything. The moon's not even out," Vivian said.

"I want to test that theory," Moss said and began swimming toward them.

"Moss, you swim one foot closer and I swear I will bloody your nose and leave you to the freshwater sharks," Giovanni said, and Moss began swimming quickly away.

Vivian dove under the water and emerged a moment later with Giovanni's trunks. "Done. Next."

"Lou, it's your game," Benny said, facing her with a smile.

She held her suit aloft and flung it onto the shore. "You're up."

He wrangled his trunks off and also tossed them toward the shore. "Vivian's right, it's so dark," he added, his tone disappointed.

"The cloud cover could lift at any time," Lou said. "It's like Russian roulette for naked people."

"Done," Moss called. "Where's Molly?"

"Far away from you, and I'm also done," she called.

"Now what?" Benny asked.

"Now we go on about our business like nothing is different," Lou said.

"Then what's the point?" Moss asked.

"The point is now when we're playing some game and the question comes up, 'Have you ever been skinny dipping,' we can all answer yes," Lou said.

"You were already able to answer yes to that," Benny reminded her.

"And now I've brought you all to my level and we'll make a competitive team. Hey, I have a question for the Samperis," she said.

"Does it involve illegal drugs or gun running? Because you can only lead us down the path of unrighteousness so far, Lou," Giovanni said.

"No, it's a real question. Who is going to be in charge when your TV show starts? Will it be Jessamine because she's the designer?" Lou said.

"Jess is not the boss of me," Moss said.

"No, that's still Mom's job," Giovanni added.

"Joe?" Lou tried.

"Joe's not like that," Benny said.

"Then who? How's it going to work?" Lou asked, and the brothers began a long and vocal debate about who was going to be in charge and how their division of labor would be separated when the new television show began. When they finally came to some sort of agreement, Moss looked around.

"Where are the women?"

"Lou's probably swimming laps," Benny said, unconcerned. Then he cocked his head. "Although it is strangely quiet."

"Yeah, it's weird Vivian would disappear without a word," Giovanni said, scanning the water. "Vivy?"

"Lou?"

"Molly?"

"Hey," Lou called from far ashore, waving. The three women stood together on the bank, their suits back on. "We're calling it a night. See y'all."

"That's weird," Giovanni said.

"Maybe they're going to get a snack," Moss said.

"No, something is definitely up. Lou never stops swimming this soon," Benny said.

"Guys, if the women were wearing their suits, what was in their hands?" Giovanni asked.

"They wouldn't," Moss said.

"Have you met them?" Benny said. He swam ashore and searched fruitlessly for their clothes. "Gone," he called.

"What are we supposed to do?" Giovanni said.

"I'm not walking through the hotel naked," Moss said. "That's like incest or something."

"Stop using words you don't know the meaning of," Giovanni commanded. "I cannot believe my wife did this to me. This is Lou's bad influence. Vivian never did anything like this until your girlfriend showed up."

"Are you talking about the Vivian who eloped with you on a whim and kept it secret from everyone for almost a year?" Benny said.

"You may have a point there," Giovanni conceded. "But, seriously, what are we going to do?"

"We're going to have to sneak up to the hotel, try to get someone's attention, and have them bring us some clothes," Benny said. "And then the women are going to pay."

"Ooh, I like that part," Moss said, rubbing his hands together in anticipatory glee.

"If Vivian thinks she's getting sex tonight, she…well, no she's probably right," Giovanni said. "I actually have no way of getting back at her."

"Remember what it was like before you were neutered?" Moss asked.

"Remember what it was like when you slept alone every night? Oh, wait, that's still happening," Giovanni said.

"Guys, we can't turn on each other. That's what they want. We have to stick together if we're going to make it back undiscovered," Benny said.

"You're just a general without a platoon, aren't you?" Moss asked him.

"Pipe down, soldier, we're going to get your pants back," Benny said. They emerged from the water and began darting from tree to tree toward the front of the hotel. It took a long time to get someone's attention and then beg for towels to be brought to them. Eventually they all made it inside, towels wrapped around their waists as if they had emerged from the shower.

They waited to take their revenge until several hours later. "We have to lull them into a false sense of complacency," Benny told Moss. "They'll think we gave up on getting revenge and go to sleep." In the meantime, he talked Sheila into giving him a key to the girls' room.

Finally, in the wee hours of the morning, they used the key, sneaked into the girls' room, and dumped a bucket of icy water on each bed.

"Wait a minute, shouldn't they be screaming?" Moss asked.

"Turn on the light," Benny commanded.

Moss did so, and they scanned the room in surprise. It was completely empty of all traces of humanity, as if no one had ever stayed there. On Lou's bed was a note. Benny picked it up and read aloud.

"We switched rooms. Better luck next time! XO, Lou and Molly."

"They're a whole other level of evil," Moss said, tossing down his empty bucket in disgust.

But Benny couldn't speak; he was laughing too hard. He would probably never get a leg up on Lou, but she made it oh, so fun to keep trying.

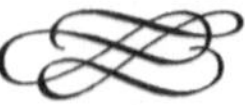

CHAPTER 24

The next morning Moss came downstairs with bright green hair. "So, you ladies had a little fun putting Kool-Aid in the showerhead, did you?" he said, his frown encompassing Vivian, Molly, and Lou.

"It was only a prank, Moss. Don't be a Grinch," Lou said.

"Ha, ha, ha, it's funny because I'm green now. I would like to remind you what they say about paybacks," Moss said.

"That they're a lot scarier if you look like Shrek?" Vivian guessed.

"Wow, you girls are digging a trench for yourselves. And now I owe you double. But Moss never forgets." He tapped his temple, but his fingers were also stained green, and the three women collapsed into fits of giggles.

"We're sorry, Moss. We know it's not easy being green," Molly said and Lou and Vivian high fived her.

Giovanni joined them and sat down. "Ladies," he said, offering them a nod. "Kermit," he added, tipping a greeting to Moss.

"You're jealous because my hair has the ability to go green. It's not all stupid black like yours. You're going to go gray soon, like Granddad."

"You're right, Moss," Giovanni said, his tone sullen. "I'm turning green with envy. Oh, wait, that's you."

"I expect as much from Lou and Vivian, but Molly, my sweet Molly, what have I ever done to you?" Moss said.

She arched an eyebrow. "Do you want an actual list?"

"On second thought, never mind," he muttered, sullenly tucking in to his giant bowl of cereal.

"Where's Benny?" Giovanni asked.

"Doing the usual Benny wrap up," Lou said. He had to talk to the pastor who had coordinated the event, say his goodbyes to Sheila, double check with Charlie to make sure everything was set for the ride home, and then make a few closing announcements.

"How does he have so much energy?" Giovanni said. "I'm exhausted."

"He doesn't," Lou said worriedly as she watched Benny buzz through the room, his physical tank clearly on empty. In other ways, he seemed steadier, more robust, as if the week had provided emotional healing. Lou couldn't help but feel like she had been a part of that, and she was glad. Whatever became of them, it had been worth it to help restore Benny back to where he should be. She had hated seeing him so close to being broken. Though tired, he now seemed rejuvenated. But rejuvenation was a double-edged sword. It meant he felt ready to go back on the road.

After breakfast, Lou helped Molly carry the luggage downstairs and said goodbye to Sheila, their hostess extraordinaire. She boarded the bus and waited for Benny to make his closing remarks. He didn't disappoint, and she thought she heard a few people sniffling by the time his inspiring speech was finished. At last he sat down and turned to look at her.

"Hattie Lou Lawton," Benny said slowly.

"Benedict Arnold Samperi."

"For the ten thousandth time in our lives, that is not my middle name," he said.

"Are you sure? Because it rolls right off the tongue," she replied.

"Mischief always does for you," he said.

"Mischief? What kind of word is that? Are you Santa now? Am I on the naughty list?"

"I hope so, but let's shelve that discussion for later," he said. "My point is the week is over. You are no longer my fake mission camp girlfriend. You are free to go, all debts are paid, and I thank you for your service."

"Why do I feel like the National Anthem should be playing?" she asked.

He squeezed her knee. "It was a good week."

"It was an excellent week, some might even say exceptional," she said.

"Those who went to Princeton might say that. Those who work construction say good. The thing is, Lou, I was thinking maybe, if you wanted, we could sort of…"

"What are you trying to say Samperi? Because this is more painful than watching you try to utter a phrase in French class freshman year," she said. "And I quote, 'jew maypelle Benny.'"

"In my defense, I only took that class because Joe told me they would teach kissing," he said.

"Apparently you picked it up by independent study," she said.

He smiled, then shook his head. "Don't derail me, this is important. The thing is, I was wondering if you might like to sort of try things in the real world."

"I don't follow," Lou said.

"Lou, would you go on a date with me?"

"Oh," she drawled. "When?"

"How's tomorrow?" he asked.

"This is all so sudden. I'm a demure Southern girl, and you're being rather forward," she said.

"I'm forward? You crawled into my bed wearing a see-through nightie," he said.

"That was a medical emergency, and it was absolutely not see through, you dirty minded lecher," she exclaimed.

He held up a finger to silence her. "Moss, come here for a minute." Moss appeared and leaned on the seat opposite them.

"What's up?" he asked.

"Was Lou's nightgown see through?" Benny asked.

"Completely," said Moss. "Thanks to you, Lou, I no longer need to read that anatomy book my mom gave me with the picture of the bee on the cover."

Lou covered her flaming face while Moss wandered back to his seat. "That gown is definitely going in the burn pile," she said.

"Are you joking? It should be enshrined. And it will be, in my mind," he said, tapping his temple. "Meanwhile you've kind of left me hanging out here on this precarious emotional branch with my heart in my hands."

"I might consider going out with you, but you should know that, as a proper Southern belle, I don't kiss on the first date," she said.

"Hmm, you're kind of making me miss my camp girlfriend," he said.

"Special, was she?" she asked.

"She was the best—super hot and unable to keep her hands off me. Kind of crazy, though."

"She sounds too good to be true. Are you sure she wasn't a figment of your imagination?"

"I have proof," he said. He took her phone and scrolled to the picture of them together.

"I'm not going to lie, she looks a little out of your league," Lou said.

"She was definitely slumming, but that's how camp goes. Lots of star-crossed love stories," he said.

She rested her head on his shoulder. "Why so glum, chum?" he asked. "And I mean that in the friend way, not the shark bait way."

"I'm feeling a little melancholy, I guess. This week was an anomaly, and it sort of feels like real life will never measure up," she said.

"I guess we'll have to try to make real life even better," he said.

"Your head must be like a Pinterest page full of inspirational quotes," she said.

"Keep your head up, kitten, hang in there," he said. "The sun will come out tomorrow."

"You're only one lawsuit away from playing the first male Annie on Broadway," she informed him.

"Bet your bottom dollar," he said.

Lou's phone chirped with a text. As she read it, her smile slipped and her expression froze.

"Everything all right?" Benny asked. "You're sort of staring into space and gripping your phone like you're about to throw it."

"You will never believe who that was from," she said.

"The President?" he guessed.

"Zel."

"Your ex-fiancé Zel?"

"One and the same."

"Does he text you often?" he asked.

"I haven't seen or spoken to him in nine years, since we broke off our engagement. What is up with this week? Was there a meeting of everyone I ever loved where you all decided to crash back into my life at once? Was the black Power Ranger there or Josh Groban?"

"You had a crush on Josh Groban?" he asked.

"He has the voice of an angel, but that's beside the point. Why is Zel texting me?"

"What did he say?" Benny asked.

"Apparently he's been thinking about me and wants to get together for coffee," she said.

"In other words he's getting the married man's seven year itch," Benny said.

She counted on her fingers. "It has been exactly seven years since they got married. And he thinks I've been standing by all this time, waiting to get back in line after they ran their course."

"What are you going to say to him?" he asked.

She stared at her phone. "I have no idea. How do you respond to that without resorting to some sort of hex or pain-inducing curse?"

"You don't have to respond. You could ignore it. You could take the high road and offer a polite refusal. Or you could hand me the phone and let me reply for you," he said.

She gave him the phone. He texted for a minute and then hit send.

"What did you say?" she asked. He gave her the phone back and she read out loud, "Hey, Zel, great to hear from you. I hope you and your wife are doing well and staying happy. My boyfriend and I would love to have coffee with you. Give me a text next time you're in town."

"I guarantee you will never hear from him again," Benny said.

"This fake boyfriend thing has all kinds of benefits," Lou said.

"Wait until you see what a real boyfriend can do for you," he said.

CHAPTER 25

The doorbell rang. Lou tried to pretend she wasn't hurrying to answer it. Benny stood on the other side, flowers in hand. "These are for you," he said, sounding as nervous as she secretly felt.

"They're so beautiful," Lou said, taking them and inhaling deeply. "They don't smell."

"That's because they don't have noses," Benny said.

"What are they? They're so pretty."

"They're dahlias. Dahlias don't have a fragrance. Also, if my mom asks, they definitely did not come from her garden and you haven't seen me."

"You stole these flowers from your mom's garden? Nice. Are we heading to Costco for some free samples in lieu of supper?" she asked.

"I didn't steal them," he argued.

"You mean I have to give them back?" she said.

"No, I mean it's community property, for the most part. But the dahlias are my mom's favorite because they're fussy, and I brought them to you because they're my favorite, too, and because flowers from a florist remind me of funerals."

"Wow, I was giving you a hard time, but you've actually thought this through," she said.

"Do you feel bad for raking me over the coals?" he asked.

"No, but I find you slightly more adorable," she said.

"Seems like a good trade, I'll take it," he said.

"Come in," she said as they both realized he was still standing on her porch. He followed her inside and closed the door.

"This place has great bones," he said, scanning the interior of the large house, a massive midcentury modern ranch with an open floor plan.

"Thank you, I thought it had character. I haven't done much decorating yet because I sort of freeze up every time I try," she said.

"You should call Jessamine, it's kind of her thing," he said.

"I did, but her secretary, who I now realize is Molly, said she was too busy."

"She makes time for family friends. She probably never got the message you called. Molly runs a lot of interference for us," he said.

"Follow me to the kitchen so I can stick these in some water," she said.

He tagged behind her to the kitchen and leaned in the doorway while she found a vase and filled it with water. When she was finished, she had nothing to do with her hands. She turned to face him, and they fluttered helplessly to her sides.

"You look incredible, Lou," he said.

"Thank you." She glanced down as if to remind herself what she was wearing. It was still the maxi skirt and spaghetti strap blouse she'd picked out. She almost always wore some version of the same outfit because the skirt was long enough to hide her braces and the shirt allowed a nice view of her well-toned upper body. Daily swimming and stretches had given her a willowy, muscular physique, though the main reason she did it was to stay limber and avoid having to go back to her wheelchair. When she looked back up again, Benny had taken several steps and was now standing directly in front of her.

"Hi," she said.

"Hi," he replied. "You seem nervous."

"So do you."

"That's because I am," he admitted.

"So am I," she agreed. "It's kind of a big deal, a first real date."

"I've already kissed you," he reminded her.

"A lot," she added.

"We've slept in the same bed," he said.

"Until your mom showed up," she said.

"I thought we agreed to never speak of that again," he said.

"You're right, sorry. And I get where you're going with this. We've been friends forever, we've already come a long way. There's no reason we should be nervous."

He picked her up and set her on the counter in front of him so they were eye level. "Let's not begin at the beginning, that's too much pressure. Let's pick up where we left off."

"Where did we leave off?' she asked.

"Right about here, I think," he said and kissed her.

"Now I remember," she said when the kiss was finished.

"I missed you like crazy today," he said.

"I had a productive day at work," she informed him. "I downloaded the picture you took of us, made it my screensaver, and stared at it for half an hour."

"That Ivy League education pays for itself every day," he said.

"It's okay, nepotism makes me unfireable," she said. She tugged him closer and kissed him. Eventually he broke away.

"I have the feeling if we don't leave now, we're never going to," he said.

"You must be starving," she said.

"I am, but I also want to talk to you about something, and it's probably best done over a nice meal. I made reservations at Jean-George."

"You are kidding me, how did you score that?" she asked. Jean-George was the nicest and most exclusive restaurant in the next town over.

"My family built it. And you know what they say, if you build it, they will give you a freestanding reservation for life."

"I didn't think you guys did commercial stuff," she said.

"We dabble. Are you ready?"

"I'm ready," she agreed. He lifted her off the counter and followed while she gathered her purse and locked the doors. Once outside, he opened the car door for her and held it while she slid in.

"Whose car is this?" she asked. He didn't own a car since his stay in the states was temporary.

"My parents. They keep it on hand for me when I come back, and sometimes Moss uses it when the ridiculous muscle car he owns goes in the shop," Benny said.

"Do you ever feel bad about the massive amount of privilege we've been handed?" she asked.

"Only every day, but I also think we both try to do the best with it we can. It's not like we're on *Rich Kids of Instagram* or drunkenly wrecking our yachts on the weekends," he said.

"That reminds me, I have to call the yacht shop and see if *The Lou* is ready to sail again," she said.

"Are you going to take her out on the crick again this weekend?" he asked.

"The other members of the Landlocked Kentucky Yacht Club and I call it 'the creek,'" she said.

They were stopped at a light. He glanced at her, smiling. "You're cute."

"And you're," she began, and then the crash came, a horrible smashing sound as the car behind them barreled into them, sliding them forward into the middle of the intersection as both airbags deployed.

For a second everything was still. Slowly, the world came back into focus. Lou's ears were ringing, but she became aware Benny was yelling at her, or maybe to her.

"Are you all right? Are you hurt?"

Was she? "I think so. Are you all right?"

"Yes. We should get out of the car, we're in the intersection," he said. He opened his door and got out. Lou opened her door, but her legs wouldn't cooperate. Benny came around and helped her out.

"Shoehorn," she noted, but her brain didn't fully connect with the comment. She still felt shocked and more than a little shaky. He led her out of the intersection and toward the vehicle that had hit them. A man sat in it, conscious but clearly drunk or high out of his mind.

Benny sighed. "Did you call 911?" he asked Lou.

"Oh, no," she said. She reached for her phone and dialed, giving their location and a description of the vehicle that hit them, as well as the license plate number. While she was on the phone, several cars stopped to check on them. A couple of people waited with them until the state trooper arrived.

"Y'all are lucky you didn't get hurt. That was a bad hit," one of their good Samaritans said.

The trooper arrived in short order, followed by an ambulance. "It's standard procedure for an accident where airbags deploy," the trooper told them as he took their information and had them fill out statements. "I strongly suggest you go to the hospital and get checked out. In drunk driving accidents, it's especially important we know if someone is injured. It could increase his penalty."

"I suppose we'd better," Benny said. "Better safe than sorry."

"At least we can share an ambulance. That's kind of romantic, right?"

Except it wasn't. Their EMT was a guy they had gone to high school with, and he alternated sympathetically examining them with teasing them over their messed up date.

"If y'all had gotten together in high school like you should have, you wouldn't be having this problem."

"Thanks, Woody, that's extremely helpful," Benny said.

"Wowzers, Lou, you grew up nice. I like your hair long now, and was it always so blond? That year in France or whatnot sure did you good. If I'da known you'd grow up to look this good, I woulda asked you out back then," Woody said.

"You do know you're saying these things out loud and we can hear you, right?" Lou said.

"And, hello, I'm sitting right here," Benny said.

"That's okay, a little competition is always healthy," Woody said.

"Yeah, it's going to be a tight race, for sure. Practically a photo finish," Lou said.

Woody chuckled. "You and your smart mouth, Lou."

"No, no, you're not allowed to talk about her mouth anymore, or any other part of her," Benny said. "How much longer until we get to the hospital? This has to be the longest ride ever."

"Y'all need to relax. You're getting riled," Woody said.

"You hear that, Ben, we're getting riled," Lou said.

"I can't imagine why," Benny said. At last they pulled into the emergency bay of the hospital and, though they wished to walk without assistance, hospital policy mandated they ride in chairs.

"It's like going back in time," Lou said grumpily. She had hoped never to ride in another wheelchair again.

"At least we're here now. The worst is over," Benny said, but that was before the orderly opened the door and he saw his entire family gathered in the waiting room.

"Did you use my phone to call them?" Lou asked.

"No," Benny said.

"How do they do that?" Lou asked.

"My mom has spies everywhere," Benny said. "Or she's psychic. I haven't figured out which one is true yet."

Benny and Lou waved at the Samperis as they were wheeled past. The sight of so many of them made Lou feel a little lonely. Her parents probably would have come, too, but they were currently out of the country.

"You're so lucky to have so much family," she told him.

"Lucky, yes, that's exactly the word I was thinking just now," Benny said.

They were wheeled to side-by-side bays with only a curtain between them. As soon as the orderlies were gone, Benny opened the curtain and hopped from his bed to Lou's. He put his arm around her.

"Are you sure you're all right?"

"I'm fine. We'll probably both be sore tomorrow, but it's nothing a tub of ice cream won't cure," Lou said. She leaned into him and rested her head on his shoulder. "How about you?"

"I'm feeling pretty good right now," he said. He was leaning in to kiss her when the outside curtain was ripped open and his parents arrived.

"Again? We can't leave you two lovebirds alone for a minute, can we?" Mrs. Samperi said.

"Apparently not," Benny said.

"How ya feelin', son?" Mr. Samperi asked. He was the smallest and loudest of the bunch. His voice boomed around the small space so Lou had to fight the urge to shrink back. His Brooklyn accent was as thick as his wife's, even after so many years in Kentucky.

"I'm fine, Dad," Benny said.

"How about you, Lou?" Mr. Samperi bellowed.

"I'm fine, too, Mr. Samperi. It's nice to see you again," she said.

"You, too," he agreed with a smile.

"I hope this puts a definitive end to the Africa nonsense," Mrs. Samperi said, and Benny froze.

"What Africa nonsense?" Lou asked.

"Ma," Benny exclaimed.

"Oh, oops," Mrs. Samperi said, looking sheepish for the first time in Lou's memory.

"That about does it, Marie. Out, out, out," Mr. Samperi said as he herded his wife back through the curtain.

"What was she talking about?" Lou asked.

Benny sat with his eyes closed, looking pained. "I got a call from UNICEF while I was gone, Lou. I was going to talk to you about it tonight. There's a crisis in the Congo. They want me to lead a team."

"When?" she asked.

"Three days," he said. "But, Lou, this is like being called up to the big leagues for a guy like me. This is what I've been working for my whole life."

"Of course you have to go," Lou said quietly.

He took her hand. "I want you to come with me."

She laughed weakly. "Benny, I just got back from vacation, I can't take another one."

"I'm not talking about a vacation. I'm talking about forever," he said.

"What?"

"I want you to move to Africa with me. We work great together, and I know you would love it there," he said.

"You want me to take a job in Africa with you?" she said.

"No, I want you to be my wife. I'm asking you to marry me. Badly, but that's what I'm saying. I love you, Lou, you have to know that. I don't want to leave you again, I don't want to lose what we have again."

"Benny, I can't go to Africa," she said.

"You could run your company remotely and come back a few times a year," he suggested.

"It's not only my company. You have four siblings, but my parents only have me. They're getting older. I can't abandon them to follow your dream. And the truth is I don't want to. I love my job, I love my home, I love our town. I don't want to uproot and move around the world," she said.

"So that's a no," he said, sounding wounded.

"It's a no to Africa," she said.

"What are you saying, you'd marry me if I stayed here?" he said.

"I would never ask you to do that," she said.

"I guess that's the difference between us because, if the situation were reversed, I would ask you to stay," he said.

"You want to know another difference between us? I wouldn't resent you, if you did. But you would resent me if I manipulated you into staying here, and we both know it," she said.

He let out a breath. "So, I guess this is it."

"I guess so," she said.

"This is not how I imagined this evening ending," he said.

"Me, neither. I didn't even get cake."

The doctor opened the curtain, and their examinations began. Lou's chest was tender, and they wheeled her away for an x-ray to check her collarbone. When she returned, Benny's older brother, Joe, sat in his place. He was a big bear of a man, and a total sweetheart. Lou had always adored him, as well as his wife, Peaches.

"I'll be your designated driver tonight, Miss Lawton," he said, smiling as he tipped an imaginary hat.

"He's not even going to say goodbye?" Lou said.

"He said if he saw you again, he wouldn't be able to go," Joe said. "I'm sorry, Lou."

"Don't be sorry, Joe. It's not your fault he Jim Jonesed you," she said.

He smiled. "It's crazy, isn't it? It's like I know he's getting me to do stuff for him, but he's so sweet about it I don't mind. He's always been that way. All the other kids would throw tantrums, but not Benny. He'd smile and we'd hand him whatever he wanted."

Joe stood patiently by while Lou was cleared for release and then helped her into his truck. "It's tall, I know," he said apologetically, as if the vehicle's height was why he was offering assistance and not her disability. She didn't want to talk about Benny more, and she was afraid to talk about Peaches, not knowing the status of their relationship. She searched about for something safe to say.

"Do you still take pictures?" she asked. "Last time I saw you, you were a budding Ansell Adams."

"I can't believe you remember, it was so long ago. I don't have a lot of time for hobbies anymore. Work is busy and, if there's ever any free time, I'm in the middle of renovating my own house."

"You should get back to it," Lou said. "I remember thinking your pictures were really good, and if you can't base your life choices on the opinion of a seventeen-year-old kid, then you're clearly doing it wrong."

He chuckled. "It's good to see you back, Lou. A long time ago Peaches told me she thought there was something between you and Benny. I said she was crazy. At some point you'd think I'd learn to stop doubting her."

"Don't tell, but Peaches was who I aspired to be when I was growing up," Lou said. At three years older, Peaches had always seemed so cool and put together. But she never lost her innate sweetness.

"You should give her a call sometime and get coffee or lunch," he urged, and it reminded Lou of when her mom tried to arrange friendships for her because she was worried Lou was lonely. Was Peaches lonely? It was hard for Lou to reconcile that image with the memory of the bright, sunny girl she had known in high school. Peaches had been the head cheerleader and homecoming queen, but so friendly and likeable no one begrudged her the positions.

"Maybe I will," Lou said. "We can talk about your mom."

Joe sputtered a laugh. "You might never get away if you bring up my mom with Peaches."

Lou could only imagine. She'd had one week with Mrs. Samperi. Peaches had had a lifetime. She had even lived with the family a while before she and Joe got married.

They reached her house. Joe came around to open her door and offer her a hand and then walked her to the door to make sure she got in okay.

"Call if you need anything, Lou. Benny said your parents are out of town, and there are always enough Samperis to go around. My mom will probably send food tomorrow because it's what she does."

"Thanks, Joe. I still claim you as the big brother I never had," she informed him.

"I'm always happy to add another little sister," he said with his signature kind smile. But behind the smile, his eyes seemed a little sad. Lou looked away. She couldn't take any more emotion tonight, and especially not from Joe, whose life should always be pleasant, if only as a reward for being so good.

Lou let herself in, ate a bowl of cereal, took some pain reliever, and went to bed.

Sometime in the night, her phone beeped with a text. She ignored it and went back to sleep. In the morning, she went for a long swim. When she emerged, her muscles felt stiff and sore. Her legs refused to go in their braces or walk without a wobble, so she pulled out her wheelchair and sat down. At last she could put it off no longer and reached for her phone to read the text she somehow knew would be from Benny.

Moss let me use his phone. Can't sleep, can't stop thinking. I meant everything I said, Lou. I want you with me. Think about it, please.

As she was reading that text, another came through.

How are you?

Sore, she replied. *You?*

The same. Mom's sending food with Moss, he'll be there soon. Did you think more about what I said? I know it was a lot to lay on you in the hospital.

Nothing has changed, she wrote. *My place is here.* She paused, debating about whether to add more. Her thumbs flew over the letters, and she hit send before she could think too much. *I love you.*

She held onto the phone for the rest of the day, but Benny never replied.

CHAPTER 26

*D*ateless. Again. For three of the four years Lou had attended the city's annual charity gala, she had gone with her father. The first year she had been in the middle of an ill-fated relationship with an accountant she met at a tax seminar. They spent the entire evening talking about which of the evening's expenses counted as write offs and then broke up almost immediately after. Until now that had been her worst memory of the gala. From now on it would be like a before and after. Before she re-fell in love with Benedict Samperi and after he chose Africa over her.

Maybe it was time to stop going to the galas. Or maybe she should get a goat. She wasn't a cat person and she wasn't a horse person, despite being in the center of horse country. She loved dogs, but never had enough time to invest in one. But goats were fairly self-sufficient. Her two-acre property was plenty big enough, and it would be easy to fence part of it off and build a small barn. Lou especially loved the fainting goats that fell over whenever they were startled.

Goats were foremost on her mind as she moseyed through the gala crowd, schmoozing with business associates she knew but didn't really *know.* It was always the same conversation and required little of Lou's full attention. Every time she came to a party such as this, she was reminded of her favorite Franklin Roosevelt story. Once, when he found himself in a similarly dead-end social situation of repeating the same inane greeting over and over, he switched it up and instead began saying, "I murdered my grandmother this morning," to everyone he met. As expected, everyone continued to gush over him, nodding and smiling except for one alert attendee who replied, "I'm sure she had it coming." What would people say if, as Lou moved from person to person and shook hands, she began to say, "I'm thinking of getting a goat, the kind that faints." Better yet, what if she brought her goat next year? That would be one way to liven things up and give her something to look forward to. She imagined her goat fainting now as the man in front of her revealed how much he had paid for his vacation home.

"Two million dollars for a lake house," he would say, and her goat would fall over in a dramatic heap at his feet. Maybe then Lou wouldn't have to smile and nod and pretend she was interested in the lake house or the extensive renovation it had needed.

Someone touched the small of her back and Lou tried not to stiffen. People were always touching her at these events, a hand on her shoulder, hip, or waist, as if it were a normal and non-intimate form of communication for near strangers. Maybe she should get a guard goat, the kind with horns and a tendency to butt people.

She turned to see who the latest Touchy McFeely was and came face to face with Benny.

"You're in Africa," she blurted, interrupting the boring man's oh-so-gripping story about pontoons.

"It would appear I'm not," Benny refuted. He turned to the dull man and shook his hand. "How do you do, Mr. Feldman. Do you mind if I steal Lou away for a minute?" He took Lou's hand without waiting for an answer, threading her through the throng of well-dressed acquaintances. Lou had no idea if she spoke to any of them or even smiled. For all she knew, she might have shoved them aside, so dazed was she.

Benny led her out of the banquet hall and around a corner to a deserted hallway.

"Hi," he said when they were finally alone.

"You're here," she said. "Aren't you? Have I finally snapped and lost it completely?"

"Yes, but I'm also really here," he said. "And I have something for you." He reached into the pocket of his tuxedo—he was wearing a tuxedo, she noted in the remote part of her brain that was still functioning—and withdrew a wrist corsage.

"You brought me a corsage? That's not exactly gala appropriate attire," she said.

"This isn't for the gala. This is the one I got you for prom fifteen years ago," he said.

"It's remarkably well-preserved," she noted as he slipped it on her wrist.

"Okay, this isn't that one, but it's a close second. I'm sorry I'm late, but consider this Prom Night 2.0."

"You're here, you got me flowers, and you're wearing a tux," she said. The other men were wearing tuxes as well, but she couldn't seem to wrap her mind around the fact Benny was in one. It was so incongruous with the dusty, spattered construction wear she had become used to.

"Are you auditioning for the role of the narrator?" he asked.

"But you left for Africa. Moss texted me you were safely in the air," she said. She remembered distinctly because she had sat at her kitchen table and consumed an entire pint of cookie dough ice cream.

"I did leave for Africa. And then I was in Heathrow, waiting for my connecting flight, when I remembered our deal. I couldn't welch on the gala, not after ditching you for prom. Plus, we pinky swore."

"You came all the way back from London for one night because we pinky swore?" she said.

He nodded. "Seeing you in this dress is worth one night, plus a thousand, plus the rest of our lives."

"What?" she said.

"I started thinking about you being an only child," he said.

"That must have been some long, boring layover," she interjected.

He put his finger to her lips. "Shut your sarcasm hole, if you want an answer to the riddle of why I'm here," he said. She pressed her lips together, and he continued. "I thought about what you said, about how it's up to you alone to take care of your parents. And I realized how unfair that was. There are five Samperis and we can still barely handle our mom. There's no way you can do it alone. What kind of best friend would I be if I let you try?"

"What?" she repeated dumbly.

"You're a little slow on the uptake tonight, but you look good enough to spread on a cracker, so I'll allow it," he said.

"Did you just compare me to cheese?" she asked.

"A fine cheese, but I'm glad you're catching up," he said.

She wasn't catching up, though, because she had never been more confused. "What is going on? You came back for the gala and you like cheese is what I'm taking away from this conversation. Also, you might have an unhealthy attachment to my parents and their future wellbeing."

He rolled his eyes. "I was being romantic."

"Unromanticize it for me, Samperi."

"I'm staying here."

"What about Africa?" she asked.

"It's still there, as far as I know," he said.

She wanted to shake him, especially because he was enjoying himself at her expense. "I'm pregnant."

"What?" he exclaimed. "How is that even possible when we never...?"

"It's not, but I wanted to bring you up to my level of confusion," she said. "Now kindly tell me what's going on."

He blinked at her, trying to bring his heart rate back to normal. "There's something seriously wrong with you."

She ran her finger down his chest. "I know. You were saying."

"I'm staying here. I finally realized I'm not well enough to travel fulltime yet," he said.

"And when you are?" she said.

"Who knows when that will be? We could have one or more kids by then," he said.

"We're having kids?"

"My mother will insist on it," he reminded her.

"So in exchange for you staying here, I have to have a baby," she said.

"I think that seems like a fair trade," he said.

"That's because you're not the one who has to push a cantaloupe through a straw," she said. "What about your job? What if you get bored staying here with me?"

"Lou, in the short time we've been together, we plunged in an elevator, got caught in a tornado, were shot at, and hit by a car. We broke into someone's house, got chased out of an abandoned barn, and went skinny-dipping. Being bored with you would be like being bored at Disneyworld while hopped up on amphetamines and caffeine—it's not going to happen."

"A week ago, you were set to go. What changed your mind?" she asked.

"Your little talk made me realize that, even though there are five of us, my family needs me, too. Maybe with me here to pick up the slack, Joe will have time to address his issues. You also showed me I can do mission work from anywhere. I don't have to be across the globe to make a difference. Maybe I could help you take the Hartwell Foundation international."

"It's already international," she said.

"You're kind of letting the wind out of my sails here," he said.

"But we're always looking to invest in new projects," she hastened to add. "Maybe you could work for me in some sort of pro bono advisory capacity."

"Pro bono?" he said.

"Well, no money would exchange hands, but I'd be willing to offer you other things," she said.

He smiled and held out his hand. "You pinky swear on it?"

"I most definitely pinky swear," she said and clasped his little finger with hers. He used his pinky to tug her hand closer and slipped a ring on her third finger.

"Did you use a pinky swear to trick me into marrying you?" she asked.

"I did, and there's no going back because a pinky swear is legally binding for Italians," he said.

"I'm not Italian," she told him.

"That's okay, I'm Italian enough for both of us," he said.

She held the ring close to inspect it. "Holy cow. Did you knock over a diamond mine in South America?"

"This is my Nonna's ring," he said.

"How did you get it?"' she asked. "Please tell me Nonna still has all her digits."

He shrugged. "She wanted me to have it."

"You Jim Jonesed your grandmother out of her ring, didn't you?" she asked.

"Are you complaining?" he asked.

"No. Do you think you could get her to give you some matching earrings?" she asked.

"I'll see what I can do," he promised and kissed her.

Thank you for reading *A False Front*, Book 2 in the Builders series. For more books, please visit my website at www.vanessagraybartal.com

www.ingramcontent.com/pod-product-compliance
Lightning Source LLC
Chambersburg PA
CBHW032029050726
47590CB00006B/2349